SUTTON ASYLUM

A DARK TABOO ROMANCE

KINSLEY KINCAID

Cover Design: 3 Crows Author Services

Editing & Proofreading: Book Witch Author Services

eBook ISBN: 978-1-7389892-4-9

Print ISBN: 978-1-7389892-5-6

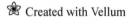 Created with Vellum

NOTE FROM THE AUTHOR

Please be aware this book contains many **dark themes** and subjects that may be uncomfortable/unsuitable for some readers. This book contains **heavy themes** throughout. Please keep this in mind when entering Sutton Asylum. Content warnings are listed on authors' social pages & website.

This book and its contents are entirely a work of fiction. Any resemblance or similarities to names, characters, organizations, places, events, incidents, or real people are entirely coincidental or used fictitiously.

If you find any genuine errors, please reach out to the author directly to correct it. Thank you.

They say if you want to tell a story right, you gotta start at the beginning.

-Harley Fucking Quinn

PROLOGUE

JASPER

AGE 15

SOUTH CAROLINA

"*Stop touching her! Stop!*"

Red. All I see is red and it will be their blood if they don't stop.

"*Let her go!*" *I'm tied to a chair in the family kitchen. In only her bra and panties, my twin sister is on the table with her arms and legs spread. Each limb has been tied down, and she is stretched out like a starfish.*

"*Iris, listen to my voice. It's going to be ok. Just concentrate on me. I'm here, I'll always be here.*"

My parents stand at her feet now that she is secure. I need to get out of this chair, but they have my hands zip-tied. Unless I can make my hands smaller to slide through, there's no way I'm getting out of this.

They caught us again. Caught us touching each other in our childhood treehouse. They'd said if we did it again, they would teach us a lesson. We believed them, but we didn't care.

Our parents have unconventional ways of punishing us. Locking one of us in the basement for days with only water and a bucket to piss and shit in. One time, father choked me until I blacked out while mother held Iris and made her watch. Making us watch the other's punishment is a new thing they have started. And it's a million times worse than the basement. I can't take it much longer. If they touch her, I'm going to fucking slaughter them when I get out of this. She. Is. Mine. Not theirs. Only I can do this to her.

Father moves his hand to her ankle, mother looks at me and smiles. These sick fucks.

"Don't. Fucking. Do. It."

Father turns his head slowly towards me and grins. My heart is racing. I can't let them do this. I need to get out of these fucking ties. I fucking hate them!

Slowly, inch by inch, his finger tip trails up her short legs. Tiny goosebumps begin to appear on her fair skin. I rock the chair around trying to distract him, but it doesn't work. He ignores my movements and keeps going. Keeps on touching what doesn't belong to him.

"We warned you. Both of you. No more touching. My stupid children, you knew the consequences would be severe, but you still didn't listen. Now it's my turn to see what all the fuss is about. What do you think, Jasper? Should daddy get to play with our precious Iris as well?"

I am seething. He can't do this. I don't show him how pissed I am. It's what he wants. My reaction. He feeds off our need for one another. Then the more we react to him, the more pain he will inflict.

"Mother thinks it's a lovely idea, don't you, mother?" His fingers caress Iris's panty covered pussy.

"Of course. The children have been naughty. They must be disciplined. Bad behavior does not get rewarded." Mother responds.

I am going to kill them.

"Do that to me. Not her. Please, not her! Pick me." I beg as a last ditch effort to stop it.

"Now, son, why would we do this to you when this is working so well?"

He's right. He is getting exactly what he wants from me. But nothing from my twin. She is still. Silent.

Not a single whimper or scream has left her mouth. A silent and still Iris is never good. They should be fucking terrified.

"Iris, my dear daughter, Daddy just wants to play, too. You are being so good for us, my sweet girl. It will all be over soon." Mother reassures her, and I see father's fingers begin to edge their way to her panty line, getting ready to reach under and touch her pussy. My fucking pussy.

That's when I hear a pop. What the fuck was that?

Looking around, I can't pinpoint where it came from. Focusing back on the table in front of me, I see my queen, my Beautiful Savage, Iris, leaning up from the table. How is this happening?

Reaching forward, she grabs father's hair tightly with her fingers and begins smashing his face into the hard wooden table.

Fuck. She must have dislocated her thumb in order to pull her tiny hand through the rope. I fucking love this girl; I think while smiling to myself.

The injury doesn't stop my Iris. She continues to slam father's face into the table. Mother is screaming but not moving. She's completely frozen in place. Mother is a follower, she won't react to what's happening unless father tells her to.

Looking back to Iris and father, I can see blood

coming from his nose. It doesn't affect her. Iris has no expression on her face other than focus and determination. I'm not shocked. When she's in the zone, nothing can break it.

After a few more, Iris lets go, and our father slides down to the tiled kitchen floor. There's blood coming from his forehead and now his mouth, too. Mother's eyes are wide, mortified at what she's just witnessed. Mother and father have never seen this side of Iris. I fucking relish it.

Iris leans back and begins to untie her other wrist, still bound by the rope, only able to use her fingers. I hope she can move fast enough before father wakes. Come on Savage, you can do this.

"I know Jasp. I'm going as fast as I can," she whispers to me while focusing on the knots.

It's our twin connection. People talk about it. Question if it's real. It is. We have it. Mind. Body. And fucking soul.

"Mother. Start on her ankle ropes. If you do this, we won't hurt you."

I need her to believe every word, so I stay as calm as I can. Mother nods her head. Of course, she complies. I don't think she has ever thought for herself. Her trembling hands move to the ties at Iris' ankles and she begins taking the knots out. By the time mother moves to the second ankle, Iris finally gets her other hand undone.

Finally, she's completely free. Iris jumps down from the kitchen table, still in only her white panties and bra. My twin's long wavy black hair is flowing over her shoulders and hanging below her nipples. She's my beautiful fucking Savage. My dick twitches at the sight of her like this.

Bare foot, Iris walks to the knife rack and finds the sharpest one. I can hear her feet against the tiles, she is behind me within seconds and cuts my zip ties free.

I rub each wrist where the ties were. They are red and sore, I can still feel them on me.

Standing up from the chair, I walk over to my father, who is just beginning to stir in the blood pooling around him from his injuries. His head turns slightly to look up at me. "Father, I told you not to touch her. I told you to leave her alone. You didn't listen. Now naughty boys that don't listen need to be punished." I smile down at him, using his own words against him. Bending over to grab him by his hair, Iris interrupts me.

"Jasper, I wanted to play with him first." Turning to look at Iris, I find her pouting, sticking her bottom lip out and giving me those big, sad cat eyes. I can never say no to her.

"Of course my beautiful Savage, you can have him all. Let me hold him for you." I offer.

She doesn't hesitate. Taking the knife, she stabs him right where his dick is, turning it slowly and he lets out a tormented scream.

"Father. We have only just begun. Hush now," Iris tsks.

"Jasp, keep him like that. He is acting like such a baby. I can't listen to him crying anymore. It's so annoying!" Removing the knife from his dick, she raises it then moves it across the skin of his neck, cutting into it like butter. I still have his hair in my hand, holding his head up, and I pull it back slightly, opening the cut more. Warm blood begins flowing out of his neck, spraying red all over my twin. She's never been more beautiful than right here in this moment with the blood of our enemy coating her body. My cock hardens against my tight, dark jeans. I fucking need her. To claim her now. But I need to focus on the task at hand. Then we will reward ourselves. It wouldn't be the first time.

"Savage, you are so strong. I'm so proud of you."

Dropping father's now lifeless body to the ground, I walk through his blood in my formerly white and black Air Force Ones, now splattered in red and stand in front of Iris.. Grabbing her face with my hands, I tilt her head up towards me and kiss her. We ravage each other as our tongues meet and we kiss as though we were each other's last meal.

Pulling back slightly, Iris whispers against my lips, "Do you hear that?" Her brown eyes shifting from left to right. I focus on the silence and that's when I hear it, too. Sirens. But how?

Letting go of my sister's face, I turn and see mother has her cellphone in her hand. We were too concerned with father. We didn't even think mother would do anything to compromise herself.

Turning back to face Iris, I can tell she's fuming, her eyes wide and nostrils flared. Grabbing the knife from my twin's hand, I walk over to our mother and without thinking or hesitation, I stab the sharp tip in her right eye, turning it slowly in a circle, then pulling it out of her face with her eyeball stuck to it. I bring it up to my face as she screams. It sounds like a mixture of pain and terror. It's feeding me to keep going. I take mother's eyeball off the knife and throw it to the floor. Never once taking my eyes off her as I do that.

"Mother. You fucked up."

Then, with minimal time to spare, as the sirens grow louder, with all my force I stab her in the heart, *then move quickly to cut her throat just as Iris did our father's. Mother's blood sprays on me as she falls to her knees. I kick her over with my foot, causing her to fall completely over. Then leave her there to choke and drown in her own blood.*

The sirens are louder now. They must be almost here. It's too late to run.

I walk back to my beautiful Savage and bring her to my chest, holding her tight. "Focus on me. It will be ok. They won't separate us. They can't separate us. We are one. We are mind, body, and soul. You are mine." Whispering into her ear as I continue to hold her petite frame covered in the warm red blood of our parents. Of our disgusting, undeserving parents.

"And you are mine, Jasper. It's us. Only ever us, always."

WELCOME LETTER

The Queen & King of Sutton Asylum
Welcome You!

One, two, do we scare you?
Three, four, lock the doors.
Five, six, can't hide behind the crucifix.
Seven, eight, we have written your fate.
Nine, ten, you better run. HA just kidding, because
you're dead!

XO
The Ashford Twins

1

JASPER

PRESENT DAY: AGE 19

SUTTON ASYLUM, SUTTON, NORTH
CAROLINA.

She is the most beautiful creature I've ever seen. Always so peaceful in her sleep, her mind at rest, if only for a few hours. It's not that I prefer her this way. I crave every fucked up version of her. But, Fuck. Ris is so beautiful like this. At my mercy.

Her long lashes are resting on her face. Straight, long black hair fanned out on her pillow with some pieces framing her delicate face.

Leaning in, she smells of the generic shower soap we are issued with a hint of mint from her toothpaste.

I watch as her chest rises with each breath. Her small breasts under her cotton nightgown moving up and down. My other half. Fuck everyone else. It's just us.

Even when mother and father tried to stop us, they couldn't. We have a bond that can never be broken. Even when death do we part, our souls will forever be one in the afterlife as they were here on earth.

Iris changed after that night. Something snapped in her brain and she's never been the same. Maybe she's more herself now. Unhinged, unpredictable and feeds off crazy. It gets her excited. And horny. Together, we rule this place. We can get anyone to do whatever we want. Out of fear. Out of manipulation. My fucking good looks and charm. Her sexuality and wildness. We intrigue and terrify. The newbs never see it coming, the vets do, but play along because they know better. I like violence, but my twin is more volatile than me. It fucking turns me on. Watching her in action. My dick gets hard just imagining it. We always get what we want.

Together we are the Queen and King of Sutton Asylum.

I slowly move my hand towards her face, brushing my thumb along her pouty bottom lip. She doesn't stir. Even in her sleep, she can feel me. I would never hurt her. Only ever protect her. Even though she doesn't need it—she's more twisted than I am.

Moving my way from her lips, I slowly caress my way down her chin, to her throat. Gently wrapping my fingers around her throat, I can feel her pulse, the tattoo between my thumb and forefinger now visible. 'MINE' permanently inked into my skin, not that either of us needs reminding who we belong to. I gave it to myself when we first got here, using pen ink and a paper clip that I shaved to a sharp point. I stole it from the nurses' desk while Ris caused a distraction. All she had to do was start laughing hysterically, and the rest joined in. The nurses hate when she does this, gets everyone riled up, especially Nurse Karen. Iris daydreams about how she would slaughter her one day. We hate Karen.

So while Karen was trying to lay the law down and threaten everyone with extra meds or solitary, not that it would work, I was stealing my supplies from her station. That night I did my first tattoo, MINE. She is fucking mine.

Whenever it starts to fade, I go over it again.

Squeezing her throat harder from the memory of that day, she still doesn't open her eyes. Iris loves this shit. Moving my other hand under her panties, I find she's soaked. I thrust three fingers into her tight pussy and start finger fucking her.

"Tighter Jasper."

I obey my queen. Tightening my fingers around her neck, her mouth opens as she tries to get air into her body. Her pussy starts squeezing my fingers when her orgasm hits, and her warm cum soaks my fingers. Her legs shake and her chest begins to convulse. She's close to blacking out now from lack of oxygen and the rush of her orgasm. Her eyes are closed, but I can see her eyes are moving rapidly underneath her lids. I continue to work her through it, Iris's hips buck a couple times before deciding to finally release her throat. Her eyes open wide as she gasps for the air her lungs desperately need. Then her legs begin to settle as her orgasm fades.

"'Such a good girl for your brother." I praise, removing my fingers from her pussy and licking them clean.

"Hmm, Jasper, I need more please," she whimpers while still trying to catch her breath.

I am not one to turn her down, ever. I pull my underwear down, remove her panties and crawl onto the bed, hovering over her. My dick is already hard and leaking precum.

Grabbing my shaft, I line it up with her pussy and rub the tip over her lips a few times.

"Jasp, please. I need you."

Wasting no time, I thrust into her. Her back arches from the rough invasion.

"Do you like my pussy, Jasp? Do you like it? How my tight pussy squeezes your big, giant cock?" Ris asks while panting harder with each thrust into her.

"Fuck, Savage, we love your tight pussy. You take us so well. So. Fucking. Well! Come on Ris, scream my fucking name when you cum all over my cock. Let the entire place know who fucking owns you."

Sitting up, she wraps her arms around my neck as I continue to drive myself into her, my tip pounding into her cervix with each thrust.

Ris brushes her lips against my ear. "I fucking own you!"

She fucking does.

I feel her breath on my neck before she bites it, then I hear the tear in my skin caused by her teeth. Pulling back slightly, she begins to lick the dripping blood off my skin. I didn't think my cock could get any harder than it already is, but it does. This shit turns me on. We both love the pain. The blood. The ownership.

Turning my head to face her, I smash my lips to hers, tasting the sweet copper flavor of my blood on her tongue. My Savage puts her hands on the back of my head, her fingers grasping my hair, and we are as close as two people can get. She moans into my mouth, and I can feel her body begin to shake with the start of her orgasm. Pounding into her harder and faster, she wraps her legs around my waist and I grab her hips for more control.

"Hmm, Jasper. You own me. Mark me as yours. Paint me with your cum."

My girl is a kinky bitch. I love when she's demanding. It sets my own orgasm into motion. My cock swells and begins shooting ribbons of cum inside of her tight pussy. Ris's warm release is still coating my cock. I work through both our orgasms. Her pussy milking me back.

"Keep milking me, Savage. My beautiful fucking Savage."

A final moan falls from her lips as our pace begins to die down, our breathing still rapid. We both rest our heads on each other's shoulders, exhausted from our fuck.

Whispering against her neck, "Yeah, I do fucking own you. As you own me, sister."

She doesn't respond. She doesn't need to. Instead raking her fingers through my wavy black hair. It's usually hanging over my forehead, but right now it's a sweaty fucking mess.

Letting go of her, I lean her back on to the bed, resting her head on her pillow. She is smiling up at me, curiosity sparkling in her eyes.

Slowly pulling out of her, I replace my cock with my fingers inside of her. Scooping our cum onto my fingers and bringing it out of her pussy.

Her smile turns into a ravenous grin. Ris sticks her tongue out, already knowing what's next. I put all three of my cum covered fingers into her mouth. She wraps her lips around me and begins sucking our release off, lapping my fingers with her tongue, careful not to miss a drop.

"How do we taste, Savage?"

Reaching her hands up, she wraps her tiny fingers around my wrist. Taking control of my hand. Ris slowly begins pulling my fingers out of her mouth, her lips swollen around them and her tongue dragging against them. Her beautiful throat moves as she swallows the last of us.

Smiling up at me, "We taste like fucking caviar, a fucking delicacy."

I crash my lips onto hers, needing a taste of what remains on her tongue. She isn't wrong, I didn't doubt her. We are mouthwatering.

"I love you, my beautiful fucking Savage. Now close those pretty eyes for me and rest. The sun will be up soon." I whisper, giving her one final kiss on her forehead.

Our room has two beds, but we only ever use one. I roll next to her and bring the blanket over both of us. Still undressed, but it isn't a sight Karen hasn't seen before when she does morning wake ups.

They usually do nightly checks, but hearing Iris's moans, because she isn't one to fuck quietly, they would know we were both in here.

Bringing Ris close to me, her eyes get heavy and she moves her head to rest on my bare chest, "Night, Jasp. Love you too."

2

IRIS

Bright eyed and freshly fucked. One of my favorite ways to start my day as Queen of Sutton Asylum. Checking myself in the wall mounted mirror with protective plastic overtop, I think of what my acceptance speech would have been if they let us have a prom here. They didn't bother to continue our education once we arrived, something about us not needing it since we were never leaving. It didn't bother us. We hated school anyway, it was so boring. But Sutton still could have given us a fucking prom!

My speech would have been something deep and meaningful. I would have let a single tear slide down my cheek, because I want my people to know how much they mean to me. Maybe it would have gone something like,

'I would like to thank the residents of Sutton for voting for me. To my devoted fans, I love you so much, I'll never let you down. And lastly, to my parents, who I despise with every inch of my beating heart, I would do it again, but better.'

Yes! That's the exact speech I would have done.

And the last bit, it's true. I would do it again. The moment father started touching me after he'd tied me to that table, I pictured killing him once I got free. His death was always going to be quick; I couldn't take being around his breathing body for another moment. He may have been the mastermind behind all our punishments and strict upbringing, but it was mother's death that I wanted to drag out more. She could have stopped it every time. She allowed my brother to be locked in the basement for days, and held me back as father beat him and choked him right in front of me. She didn't stop any of it. Mother just followed father like a brainless sheep.

I still can't believe she called the police. Color me impressed that moments before her death is when she decides to use that useless brain inside her thick skull. Once we heard the sirens approaching, everything changed and my Jasper was magnificent. He really has a knack for killing.

But I still want a redo. If I had the time, it would have been so amazing.

Jasper would have held her while I sliced all her clothes off. Then mother would have taken my place, tied down to that wooden kitchen table. I would have taken the same blood-soaked knife we used on father, and stabbed the sharp end up into her old, loose cunt. Mother's screams would have been a symphony to my ears. After rotating the knife inside of her, I would have slowly pulled it out, so that she felt every bit of the pain I was inflicting.

Next, I would have taken Jasper's brilliant idea of removing her eyes, but I would take both. Mother doesn't need to see to know what we are doing to her, plus it would just heighten her other senses. Once both eyes were gone, I would hand the knife over to Jasp so he could have some fun with mother. Jasper has the same distaste for mother as I do. I wouldn't take the opportunity from him to destroy her. Hmm, he would have definitely carved something into her, maybe an upside down cross and *'coward'* on her disgustingly saggy tits. Maybe even cutting her nipples off, adding an artistic flare.

Ah, then, before the grand finale, we both would have cut one of her wrists and watched her slowly bleed out.

I'm not sure how long it takes for someone to bleed out, but I assume watching and waiting for someone to die slowly would be terribly boring. So *the* grand finale... drum roll, please! Jasper and I would have fucked over their bodies while coated in their warm, thick red blood. We would have been so goddamn loud, making sure we would be the last thing she heard before meeting her maker.

This is why I need a do-over. It would have been fucking magical!

Picturing it makes my pussy drip.

"You look fucking delicious Savage," hearing my twin breaks up my daydream. But that's ok, seeing him standing behind me, smiling at me through the mirror and it gets my panties soaked. He is so fucking delicious. He is taller than me and has muscles I love to touch, especially while I'm riding his cock. When it comes to Jasper, I can never get enough. I crave him like a drug addict craves their next hit.

He's wearing a long white t-shirt, tight black jeans with a few holes in them, his Air Jordans and his black wavy hair hangs over his forehead. I love when he smiles, he only smiles for me. Jasper has the most beautiful smile. It shows off his perfectly straight white teeth and his cute dimples that I love putting my finger on. Biting my lip, I'm basically undressing him with my eyes. He knows. It's something I do a lot. Ugh. Sexual frustration at its finest.

"Savage, I will take care of you later. Don't worry. First, breakfast."

Turning around, I see he's reaching his hand out to me, his MINE tattoo visible, along with my name on his knuckles. He does them himself, and I love watching him do it. He is so talented. It pisses me off that I can't get him a real tattoo machine, but apparently it would be a '*safety risk*' and is considered '*a weapon*'.

Fucking hate Karen.

Don't worry, you will get the displeasure of meeting her soon.

I won't let her ruin my freshly fucked mood, though. This mood is sacred and must be protected. I only get this kind of joy a few times a day, and she will not take it from me. Karen is a stupid cunt!

If I had to rank my moods, besides my 'urge to just kill them all mood', freshly fucked would be my favorite. Thinking of all of this makes me squeal with excitement. See, Karen, you won't bring me down.

Focus Iris, food then fucking Jasper again, who is still standing behind me, chuckling and looking fine as hell doing so. I check my outfit one last time in the mirror before turning around; I'm in a white t-shirt that I had Jasper tear into a crop top because, you guessed it, Karen won't let us have fucking scissors either. Anyway, back to my fabulous outfit, I have paired it with black high waisted jean shorts and my matching black and white Air Jordans.

Satisfied with everything, I turn around and skip over to Jasper, my long black hair swaying from side to side, and grab his hand in mine, then go on my tippy-toes to kiss his sexy, dimpled cheek.

Before we go, let's address the elephant in the room. I know what you're thinking. So, I'll just say it, How do we afford to stay so fresh while in Sutton? Well, hold on folks, because you would have never guessed this!

Even though we slaughtered our parents with pride and have no regret, we were still entitled to their money once we turned eighteen. The government had to give it to us. Isn't that fucking hilarious? We got millions! Millions!

Now how mother and father acquired millions working for a culty church is a mystery I will not question. But that's how we afford the things we need, like toiletries, stuff for our room, clothes, or extras they sell at the concession.

"Savage, focus for me. Let's go eat. Plus, Dex is

waiting for you." Jasper coaxes me out of my thoughts.

His words cause my eyes to immediately light up.

Dex is my pet. My sweet baby boy.

He is the most loving, caring, loyal boy a girl could ask for. Since that day, two years ago, when I found him outside under the tree hiding from the rain, I just knew I had to have him. Dex is my favorite. Mother always said never to pick favorites, she could never have a favorite between Jasper and I. Which is true, she didn't like either of us. But what does she know? Mother did end up dead after all.

Freshly fucked, imagining prom, knowing I'll be dicked again soon, plus knowing Dex is waiting for me, makes me the luckiest girl alive.

"Well then, let's go!" I shout, rushing at my brother now.

I miss my Dexy. He needs his Mama. My excitement makes Jasp laugh while he leads me out of our room to the dining area.

Hand in hand, we walk down the hall where dark wood floors creek with each step.

After we pass a couple of other rooms, Hugo, another resident, sticks his head out of his door frame. Hugo isn't allowed a door, just a door frame lined in metal for 'safety' reasons. That's this place's go-to excuse when saying we can't have things or if we ask questions, like, *why does Hugo have a door frame lined in metal?* I later found out that he used to destroy the wood frames during his outbursts. According to another resident, he gets overstimulated easily. Sutton decided that replacing it with metal would eliminate that issue and the additional cost of repairing the wood all the time. Now he just dents the door frame. It's actually really pretty; you can see the outline of his face in a few spots if you look at it just right.

"Iris, you smell delightful. Are you wearing that new perfume again… What is it called now? Freshly fucked?" Hugo asks.

"Yes! Thank you so much for noticing, Mr. H!" I like calling him that. He seems like a man who would like formalities.

"Jasper, you are a lucky man."

"You have no fucking idea, H. You want us to do another show for you this week?" Jasper offers. Hugo doesn't leave his room. He is allowed to, he just chooses not to. Sometimes I wish he would, we would have the best time together. I just know it.

Also, show is code for fucking. We have to use code words sometimes because of fucking Karen.

We tried to fuck in front of Mr. H's door during

the day once when we first found out he liked watching, he is our neighbor after all. Wouldn't you want to know everything about yours if you could?

But fucking Karen cock-blocked us. "No fucking in the hallways!" she said in her ear-murdering voice. So now we have to wait until after lights out. We sneak into the hallway, already naked. Jasper will shove my panties in my mouth to muffle my moans while bending me over and fucking me against the wall in front of Mr. H's door. It's one of my favorite spots to fuck. The wallpaper in the hallway is soft against my hands; it's a dark green velvety material with artistic cracks throughout, which has this brown color background creeping through them. I should write a thank-you letter to whoever decided to use this wallpaper, my hands appreciate them. The lighting is also perfect. The moon shines through the window at the end of the hallway, hitting us perfectly. Almost like a spotlight.

Anyway, while Jasper and I fuck, Mr. H watches and jerks off onto his dinner, which the aides brought him earlier in the day. If it's a special show night, he saves it for us.

I'm pretty sure he eats it after we leave, which is ok, I don't judge. I think it adds more flavor to the dish. Jasper's cum would, so it's very possible Mr. H's cum does that too.

"Ah, I would love that, Jasper, my man. You two are true friends indeed. I will get back to you later on which day is best for me. I am very busy, as you know."

"You got it. See you around, H," Jasper waves as we continue down the hall.

I should point out Sutton isn't your typical asylum for the deranged and *'out of touch with reality humans'* as the good doctor likes to call us.

Sutton is an old Victorian white mansion surrounded by trees and wildflowers, and is located on the outskirts of Sutton, North Carolina.

This really old lady donated her mansion to the state when she died like a million or so years ago to use as an asylum. To the average person driving by, they would never know we were all inside. From the inside, it's certifiable. The exits have extra security, so we don't accidentally walk out. They put these really cool looking jail bar sliding doors just before the giant wood doors on the inside, so no accidental leaving happens. The windows are bullet proof glass so we can't break them and slide out in the night. Not that I have ever thought about it, of course. And you can only slide the windows up two inches for fresh air. Accidental leaving - poof! Not ever happening.

We are allowed outside time. Backyard only, and it's surrounded by a tall cagey fence with barbed wire at the top. The backyard is where I found my baby, Dex.

I tug on my brother's hand. "Jasper ,hurry up. We have to go see my Dexy!"

Jasper's free hand connects with my ass. "Well, what's the hold up? Let's go, Savage."

This causes me to squeal, I love when he spanks me. Good girl or bad girl spanks are always welcomed on this booty.

Leading us down the rest of the second-floor hallway, I rush us down the wooden grand staircase to the massive entryway on the main floor. The main floor has the kitchen, library, dining hall, art room, and TV room. Down long hallways, there's a secure ward and the primary doctor's office and his resident counseling room. Being an old Victorian house, everything is in separate rooms. They did build out the nurses' station, meds area and concession towards the back entrance, which can look into the TV room. That's where most residents spend their time during the day. The kitchen is off limits to us. It has a door that can only open with this cool badge system that beeps and flashes green when it's clear to enter. The only other door with high security is the basement. It has multiple padlocks on it. That's where you can find solitary and punishment rooms. We get sent there if we don't listen or if we act out.

Jasper and I have both been down there, separately and together. The first couple times Jasper was sent down, it reminded me of when mother and father would shove him in the basement. Keeping him away from me. They are no better than mother and father were.

Jasper and I have talked about it and if given the chance to get revenge on this place, we would take it. We aren't sure how, it would depend on the circumstance, but we would reign terror on these fuckers.

But let's not spoil the day! It's breakfast time.

Walking toward the dining hall, I smell delicious pancakes with warm maple syrup and bacon. It makes my mouth water. Tugging at Jasper's hand again, pulling him behind me, I plead for him to hurry by giving him my sad kitty eyes and pouty lips. He knows I hate missing breakfast, but he just laughs.

"Ris, if you miss anything, I will skin the cooks alive for you. I swear it."

He is so romantic.

Entering the hall, I scan the room, looking at all

the small, four-person wood tables. They are nailed down to the floors along with the wooden chairs. They nail everything down so we don't try using them as weapons. How boring, I know. I find my Dexy sitting at our table in the back corner. The windows have morning sun shining through and vintage, distressed white and brown wallpaper line the walls. But nevermind that right now, because I need to get to my boy.

"Dexy!" I shout as I rush over, throwing my arms around his neck from behind him. He leans into me and cuddles back.

"Mama missed her boy all night. Did you sleep ok?"

Dex nods and rubs his head against my shoulder. He is such a good boy. Dexy doesn't really speak. He will call me Mama, but the rest of the time it's head and hand gestures to communicate with Jasper and I. We are his protectors, not that he needs it, but because his inability to speak it makes him an easy target. We do not put up with that shit. We will fucking filet anyone who picks on Dexy.

Jasper comes up behind me, breaking up my thoughts. "Stay here while I grab our plates."

"Thank you Jasp," leaning over and giving him a quick peck on the cheek.

I give Dex one final squeeze before letting go to sit down next to him. Jasper isn't long, coming back with two plastic plates and sporks.

Ugh, my brain did it again. I wish that one day what I smelt walking towards the hall was real, instead what I see coming towards me is just toast, eggs and an apple. No coffee, just watered down orange juice. One day I'll get my dream breakfast, I just know it!

The three of us eat in silence. Various nurses are lurking, but we refuse to give them any ammo. They love when we fuck up. Pouncing on it, like they are the heroes saving the day. But they aren't. They are just really fucking annoying. So, if we need to communicate anything important while in here we will use signals with our eyes or kick each other's shins.

After taking a couple more bites of breakfast, we finish and Dex takes all three of our plates to the dirty bin. Jasper and I get up to follow when good old cunty head nurse Karen walks in shouting, "Jasper, therapy. Now!"

Karen is new. Karen also knows better. Dumb cunt.

We go together. We are not separated. We are one.

"Hey Karen. Fuck you," Jasper yells back while saluting her.

Karen has been trying to separate us since starting here a month ago. First she just observed us. Her eyes were calculated and shifty. Typical Karen behavior. Then she would try to have 'a word' with me or Jasp separately with her fake smile and frizzy fringe. We would flip her off and keep walking each time.

Finally, Karen would insert herself between us, physically blocking us from each other.

To divide us and then try to conquer Sutton will never work. She will never win whatever game she is playing at. And then she brought her bff Susan in as her backup. Susan is the last person I would ever call for backup. Karen can actually go back from wherever she came from. Shoo fly, stop bothering us.

Dex now walks back to us and stands in front of me as a form of protection. I rub his back, letting him know I appreciate it, but that it's also ok. I can handle myself.

He doesn't move, which means he is sending Karen a message as well. This is the first time he has publicly taken a stance against her.

"You three do not intimidate or scare me." Oh, Karen. But you should be.

Someone is feeling feisty today. Push me Karen, I dare you.

Sticking my head out from behind Dex so I can get in on this excitement too, "Karen, you look lovely today. You remind me of those dogs with the saggy jowls."

The other residents that are still in the dining hall gasp at first, but then start laughing. I want to take a bow for my audience, but I must focus because Jasper is stepping toward Karen, closing the distance between them.

I can't help it, I start clapping. This is getting good!

"Don't fucking demand shit from me or us again. We tell you when it's therapy. We tell you when to fuck off, then you fuck off. We run this place, not you. It would be wise for you to fucking remember that, Karen." Jasper spits at her. I can't see his face, but I know his eyes are screaming 'I will kill you if you don't listen'. She should really take the hint.

But, being above average stupid, Karen doesn't move.

"Step the fuck aside, Karen. We have shit to do." He barks at her.

Karen stands there, defiant. She is definitely trying to

prove her authority, but it's no use. The last head nurse got taken out on a stretcher. Not because we killed her, even though I wanted to, but because she tried this routine too and we didn't take kindly to it. I think the good doctor would say she suffered severe emotional and mental trauma. Jasper may have stolen the spork from the dining hall, sharpened it and held it to her throat.

Minor detail.

So, that's how we ended up in the basement that time. I may have held her arms back as he held the shank to her. Dex also may have blocked the room entrance with his body.

Just another day here at Sutton. And I say we *may* have done these things because our lawyer always said never admit fault, never admit guilt. So this *may* have happened, it may not have. But hypothetically speaking, it's a solid plan if we were to do something like this.

We are staring at Karen, unwilling to stand down, and neither does Karen until the good doc walks in right on cue.

"Ashfords, you're late!"

I knew it! She was trying to separate and isolate us. Nice fucking try, bitch. It is a twin session, not individual.

"Yeah, Karen, we are late. Step aside," I chime in, smiling at her.

She doesn't want to move, but to publicly defy the good doctor and his ultimate authority over her could only land her in one place - the unemployment line. So, like the puppet she is right now, Karen steps to the side, clearing our path.

"See, Karen, was that so hard now?" Jasper chirps.

Doc snaps his fingers at us, scowling now. "Enough you two, let's go."

Jasper grabs my hand as Dex steps aside and we follow Doc to his office. Sometimes Dex comes with us, sometimes he doesn't.

This time, I give him the look. He knows to stay and keep an eye on Karen. She's getting more bold. She's a sneaky bitch.

Dexy nods his understanding and whispers, "Mama."

Smiling back at him, Jasper and I leave the hall to start our appointment.

3

JASPER

I'm glad Ris got Dex to stay behind this time. Karen is really starting to fucking test me. She also trained her assistant head nurse to act the exact same way. I think her real name is Nancy or Beth, but who the fuck cares? We call her Susan. She acts like a Susan; therefore, she is a Susan.

The two of them are trying to challenge our authority in our own home. We live here. We run this place. And it looks like we may have to remind these two bitches about that.

Has no one in this fucking place told them about what happened to the last nurse who tried this shit? If they know and are ignoring it... Well fuck, maybe they should become residents here because they are fucking crazy if they think they will win.

The other residents bow down to my Savage,

worship the fucking ground she walks on. My beautiful Savage, my queen of the crazy. If she calls for war, Susan, Karen and anyone else in their goddamn army are done. Bodies never to be found.

I've been itching to slice up Karen. Take her down to the same basement she kept me in for four days. Four fucking days apart from the other half of my dark soul. That will never be forgiven or forgotten. They thought they were punishing me, but they were only fueling my fucking urges.

My sister and I were sent to the basement, and put in separate rooms of solitary after the spork-shank incident. No lights, they played loud music, and we only got food periodically.

They kept Dex upstairs in the hope that they could brainwash him into thinking we were the evil in Sutton. But keeping him away from Ris, his 'Mama' only pissed him off, and they ended up having to sedate him for most of our punishment. He was destroying everything, trying to get to her.

The most recent stint I did was alone. The three of us had been in the library when I heard a shit load of shouting coming from another room. Ris was reading to Dex, so I told her to stay and I would check it out.

Turns out a resident was refusing to take his evening meds and stormed off to the TV room. Susan thought it would be a brilliant idea to shut the TV off during the season finale of Grey's in order to get this resident to listen. Punish all instead of the one.

Wrong fucking decision, Susan.

I walked into the TV room, grabbed the potted plant from the floor and threw it at her head. Sadly, she moved before it would have connected with her face. But a couple of the male aides came running in, and they took me directly to solitary in the basement.

I was ok. I knew Savage had Dex with her. She wasn't alone and I could stick it out for the four days. Don't get me wrong, it killed me to be apart from her. She is my priority. But the basement punishments my father would enforce were a hundred times worse.

Here we had female aides and when they would come down to drop off food and shit, they would give me updates on my girl. I can usually get them to do whatever I want.

It's easy. I'm the bad boy of Sutton. Ris calls me the king to her queen. Chicks dig the bad boy. Give them a smirk, show off my dimples, and it instantly wets her panties. Add a bit of sweet talk and a wink, and I get what I need. It's too fucking easy some-times. When my father would punish me, I had no updates. It was hell. Fuck, enough of that depressing shit. Focusing back on the doctor and Ris, we continue walking down the hall when he speaks up. "Once we get to my office, I want to discuss the circumstances of what landed you here at Sutton. I will not tolerate a repeat of that here or a repeat of the spork incident. I am not fucking blind. I have cameras everywhere. You two are toeing the fucking line."

Oh Doc is pissed, seething even. I keep my face neutral. Ris reacts enough for the both of us and I love her for it.

"Doctor Peters, I'm hurt. I have no idea what you are implying, but I can assure you my brother and I are up to nothing but living a peaceful life," Ris bats her eyelashes even though Doc can't see since he is walking ahead of us. Doc just shakes his head and Ris shrugs her shoulders in return, causing me to laugh. I muffle it with my hand, not wanting to piss him off more than I have. But fuck, is she cute.

Doc ultimately has the final say with anything at Sutton; he is in charge of this fucking place. He signs off on all punishments, restrictions and whatever else. Susan was the reason I got sent to the basement, but Doc signed off on keeping me down there to teach me a lesson. He did nothing wrong in my opinion, but Susan did by provoking me. That cunt faced bitch crossed the fucking line. I wish that fucking potted plant would have hit her in the face. Seeing her face bloodied and cut up would have made it worth the four days.

We walk the rest of the way to his office in silence. The office is located at the other end of the home. We have to go back through the main entryway and down several long hallways to get there. Finally reaching it, he opens the door and we follow him in.

We know the drill, both taking a seat on his beige couch. Doc sits across from us in his brown armchair. Savage thinks he's handsome. I don't fucking get it. For the record, I am not threatened or jealous by Doc in any way. I own that girl and she owns me.

Doc is built, which is impressive for an older guy, and he dresses casually in blue jeans, white sneakers, and a black polo shirt. With short black hair that has a bit of a wave to it and a neatly trimmed beard, both with a little gray in them, but I am sure that just adds to his allure. He has metal wire-framed glasses, which I'm sure is a prerequisite to becoming a doctor, must wear glasses in order to come across smarter. Doc is legit, though. He doesn't need the glasses, but I won't be telling him that.

Ris clears her throat to get Doc's attention. "Doctor Peters, or may I call you Henry?"

"Iris, you know the answer. It's the same answer every time, it's Doctor Peters."

I commend her, she's persistent.

Doc blows out a breath. "You two are under my care. Under the care of Sutton Asylum for the rest of your lives. You are never leaving. It would make your stay here a whole lot easier if you participated in the program and stopped resisting and challenging authority. We only want the best for you."

"Doctor, Karen is a bitch. Susan is a cunt. Do you think maybe they need a program too?" Ris questions.

It is taking every ounce of effort in me to not laugh right now. Savage says this with the straightest, most serious face. Looking over to Doc, I think he could be on the verge of having an aneurysm, like his eyes could literally pop out of his head any second now. Ris ignores that and continues, "Also, Doctor Peters, Henry, if I may. If you cared so much about our stay and care here, then why am I never given pancakes with warm maple syrup and bacon for breakfast?"

Fuck, I love this girl. Not stopping myself, I lean forward and start laughing. Ris is an incredible woman.

Doc pinches the bridge of his nose. He's speechless. I know Doc; she leaves me speechless all the time but in the best possible ways and it usually involves her mouth and my cock.

"Jasper, sit the fuck up and stop laughing. Iris, for the last fucking time, it's Doctor Peters!"

Ris gets all pouty on him. Men can't stand seeing her upset. Well, unless it was father, he got off on that shit. So, she killed him.

I compose myself and wait for the rest of the lecture.

"You both are here because you were found unfit to stand trial, which I concluded after evaluating both of you, and the judge agreed. You would have also been a harm to the prison population when convicted. Not if convicted, *when*. You were holding each other while covered in your parents' blood when the police showed up. Their bodies lay lifeless and murdered on the floor. No remorse from either of you. And after spending the last four years with you both, I can confidently say remorse is not an emotion either of you have. You threaten the lives of anyone who tries to stand up to you. Neither of you care about what the effect of doing this could have on someone else. Not to mention the *multiple* violent acts against staff you have committed. I have had enough of it. I will fucking medicate both of you to the point where you feel like zombies. Brains occupying a body. Do you understand?" Doc spits at us.

He is not fucking around. He doesn't normally

bring up that night; it triggers Savage. He has threatened more meds on us before too when we've gotten in trouble. He never follows through, so that doesn't worry me. He knows we won't take them or if they force us, we will just throw them up. We 'take' the minimum required amount of mood stabilizers. Does he not realize how much worse it could be for him here?

We keep this place in line so riots don't occur following every outburst from any one of the other residents.

His lips part again. Apparently, he isn't done. "Also, her name is not Susan. Nurse Beth is not a cunt and Nurse Karen is not a bitch. They are just doing their jobs, which both of you and Dex are making incredibly hard for them to do."

"You leave Dex out of this!" Iris fights back. You do not bring up Dex to her in a negative way. She will throat punch any person who does. I'm shocked she is still sitting to be honest, bringing up that night, plus Dex, she has to be vibrating inside.

"He is as much a part of this as the two of you." Doc shoots back.

Fuck, I need to defuse this before Savage gets herself thrown in the basement. "Doc. Enough. We get it. You want us to play nice with Karen and Susan.

Is that all? Can we go now?" I interject before Ris does something that will land her in the basement. She would be entirely alone down there; it's happened before. And I know she's a strong fucking person, but it would kill me to have her down there.

"For now. I have you scheduled in three days from now. Same time. Don't. Be. Late. Now go," Doc dismisses us.

"Thank you for your time, Henry. Until next time." That's my beautiful Savage. She knows what she's doing, and it's brilliant to watch her work.

"GO!"

I grab my twin's hand as I stand up, and she follows my lead and we leave his office, closing the door behind us. The second I hear the latch on the door connect, I pin Savage against the wall, grip her tiny throat with my hand and whisper against her lips, "You were fucking incredible in there Savage," then smash my lips onto hers. Devouring her as she grabs the front of my t-shirt to pull me closer. My dick is hard, pressing against the fabric of my jeans. I grip her neck tighter, which makes her moan and her back arch. We love this shit.

Ris pulls back slightly, breaking our kiss. "This is going to be fun," giggling with a sinister smile.

"The best fucking time, Savage."

4

IRIS

I'm pissed. I'm giggling on the outside because I'm excited to bring both those bitches to their knees. But inside, all I feel is pure fucking rage. Henry never brings Dex up to me. In all the years he has been *'treating'* us, he has done it once before and learnt his fucking lesson. I broke a few of his fingers. Shockingly, I know, he sent me to the basement for that. He also rambled on about being proud to see I was growing an attachment to someone other than my twin and letting someone else in was a *'healthy'* step. It wasn't just bringing Dex up that bothered me during that session years ago. It was when Henry asked if Dex had shared with me the circumstances of his arrival to Sutton. Of course he hadn't, and I hadn't asked. It didn't and still doesn't matter to me. He is mine, I am his Mama and I will

49

protect him until death. How dare Henry taunt me with Dexy's pain and trauma. All I saw was red. People don't come here because life on the outside was rainbows and mother fucking sunshine. Henry pushed my last fucking button that day and his fingers felt it.

It did peak Jasper's curiosity, though. I felt it. I saw it in his face as I was being taken to solitary that day. To others, his face would appear neutral, but his eyes showed me that a part of him wanted to know. Jasper had never pressured me to find out or questioned why Dex was here. I accepted Dex, therefore, as an extension of me, so did Jasp. They get along amazingly. Their relationship is more like brothers. I love watching them together. Sometimes it's just a gesture or simple eye contact and they both end up laughing. Their own language, kinda like Jasper and me, with our twin bond. Regardless, the three of us can never be broken as long as we are together. I protect them; they protect me. We protect each other.

A few nights later, after finally being let out, I was laying in bed waiting for Jasper. It's hard to sleep without him. I get bored or restless and demons come

into my dreams at night when he isn't next to me, keeping them at bay. The nights when they separate us are always the worst.

Turning off our bathroom light, Jasp climbed into bed with me. Something felt off. He was hiding something. Waiting for him to break the silence, he blew out a sigh and said, "Savage, I got some information about Dex. Don't be mad. But after the doc brought it up, I got curious"

Deep down I had been curious too, but I have always felt it was Dexy's story to tell me. Dex hadn't spoken since arriving, other than when he whispers, 'Mama' to me. My sweet boy walks with a tortured soul.

I didn't respond to Jasper, letting him continue.

"I ran into that aide, the one with the big tits who always winks at me. Desperate bitch. Anyway, I told her, if she got me into the doc's office when he was gone, I would let her suck my cock. She was all over it. That's what I did while you were downstairs."

He let that bitch suck MY cock!

"You let her touch you!"

"No, no, that came out wrong, Savage. No. That desperate bitch didn't lay a finger on me," explaining as he cupped my face to calm me down.

I nodded, trying to calm down.

"I saw Dex's file. I know why he's here."

Tears well in my eyes. Ignoring how big tits got him access to the office. That didn't matter.

Contemplating if this is information I need, I decide it is.

"Yeah, ok. I think I can handle it. Tell me, just tell me Jasp," whispering to my twin.

"Ris, you thought we had it bad. Dex. Dex has been through shit not even I could imagine."

"Jasp, what... What happened to my Dexy?"

"His older sister... his older sister used to... rape him. It started when he was twelve, she was fifteen. It finally stopped once he killed her when he turned eighteen. His file says she would do it every night in his bed. She would sneak in and fucking rape him every night, and he took it because that was his big sister. His big fucking sister ,who should have protected him. Instead, she fucking violated him." Jasper snapped. He loves Dex as much as I do.

I had never seen my brother like this, other than with me, after our parents would discipline us. His body was vibrating under my touch.

Not even noticing until now that tears had already started streaming down my face hearing this. I can't imagine, I don't want to imagine it. If she wasn't dead,

I would have broken out of here and killed her a hundred times over.

"*How did he kill her? What happened?*" *I needed to know everything. I needed to know she got what she fucking deserved.*

"*Fuck. Ok,*" *he says, taking a breath before continuing.*

"*I guess he finally snapped one night, right before coming here. It said they found her hogtied on his bedroom floor. He was ready for her that night. He had everything he needed to end it. A cloth shoved in her mouth. Ropes to tie her with. The tools to end the pain. Dex skinned her alive. There were razor blades found all around her. And a shaver with the safety removed. He must have used that to skin her slowly, switching the blades out as they got too dull. The webbing between her fingers and toes were also cut. Along with her eyelids, gone. She had to have watched the entire thing, or at least most of it, before passing out. He inflicted his pain back on her. He got his revenge. The file said she ultimately died of shock and blood loss. He must have been at it all night, Savage. In the morning his parents found her, then him. He was in the bathtub covered in her blood shaking, holding his head and shaking.*"

My baby boy. My sweet Dexy.

Snuggling closer to Jasper, "How long after that did he come here?"

The day he arrived, I found him under the tree in the rain in Sutton's backyard. He looked so lost. I had to have him. Had to keep him. There was a natural maternal instinct to protect him the moment I saw him. Dex was in a black hoodie, with the hood up covering his short dark hair, blue jeans and white sneakers. Most people would say brown eyes are boring. Not his. Dex's eyes told me a story of strength and sadness. Tortured but vulnerable. I just didn't know how deep his sadness and hurt went.

"A few days. That day you saw him under the tree. He was still processing everything, I'm sure of it."

Nodding into Jasper's chest, I took it all in. Slowly absorbing all this horrific information. Dexy is safe now. He has me. I will always take care of him. Always.

Learning this never changed how I viewed or treated my Dexy. If anything, in some sick fucking way, our pasts brought us together. We were destined.

The next morning, after Jasper told me every-thing, we were in the library where book shelves lined the room from floor to ceiling. It had dark hardwood, like the rest of the place, with an emerald green rug.

It screamed an old Victorian gothic library. It was just us three in there.

Unable to keep secrets from him, I had to tell Dex we knew.

Dexy sat up from where he was on the floor and moved next to me on the dark purple velvet covered couch. He put his head on my lap and took one hand into mine. I used my other hand to massage his head. Comforting him for as long as he needed. I didn't let go of his hand until he let go of mine. His body shook for a while. The memory of it all surely haunts him. My poor baby. Before he let go of me, after what had to have been hours, he whispered, 'Mama.' That's all I needed to know he would be ok. We would be ok. As long as we stick together, we will get through anything Sutton has to throw at us. And we have.

I wanted to kiss his forehead. To show him he is loved. But I was also aware that it could be something that set him off, considering his past traumas. I didn't want to push a boundary with my Dexy. He would lead the physical affection with us and I would follow.

Since then, years ago now, he has gotten pretty good with it. I can run up to him and give him the biggest hugs and he doesn't hesitate. Sometimes I refer to him as my pet, the way he protects me. Dexy can sense it before we even know it's happening. Immediately on alert. Lately he's been more so, with Karen and Susan lurking, pushing our buttons and testing what they can try to get away with.

Most of the time I call him my baby boy, my Dexy.

But I often wonder now if he was born with this gut instinct, or if he learnt it from having to be on alert all those nights with his sister? Wondering when she would come in. What she would do. Mentally preparing and shutting off in order to get through to another day. For years, this happened. I know what mother and father's games and punishments did to me and Jasp. So I guess it's no wonder Dex is the way he is. I will destroy anyone who speaks his name. Anyone who thinks they have a right to judge. Fucking. End. Them.

And I know Jasper feels the same way.

We will do anything for Dexy. My perfect, fierce, sweet, broken boy.

5

JASPER

R is was pissed after we left Doc's office.

Her *'I'm going to fucking destroy the world'* giggle gave it away. Fuck, she's incredible. There is a storm brewing inside of her and I will help her roll it out whenever she's ready. You cannot fuck with what's mine and think I will sit by silently. I will destroy the world alongside her. Hell, I will even do the honors of destroying it on her behalf if she lets me. I crave the blood as much as she does, even if I don't express it the same way as she does.

Savage was in her head about something the entire way to see Dex. Doc never brings him up anymore. Not after she broke a few of his fingers. She's his Mama, their bond is as strong as ours. To bring Dex up to her in that kind of situation or atmosphere, you are asking for death. I suspect those two bitches put the idea in Doc's head. It's the only explanation. Everything was fine until they arrived. He was fine until they arrived.

I never thought ugly tits and cottage cheese pussy would fool the guy. Maybe he actually does need his glasses, and he isn't really that smart. Who knew?

Doc seemed like a decent guy. He understands who we are, and to not to cross the fucking line.

I can't understand why he just tried. We are fucking 'crazy' according to the state. We are never leaving Sutton. To try to really treat us is a declaration that they are going to try to control us. As long as Ris and I are here, that will not fucking happen.

We own Sutton.

We will make that fucking clear at breakfast tomorrow. Do not fuck with us or our home. Which includes everyone who lives here. We defend and stand up for our own.

Once we find Dex, he confirms that Karen and Susan hadn't done anything while we were gone. Ris and I stayed in the TV room for a couple of hours, wanting to see if they would do anything else today. They didn't. They were wise in keeping their distance.

I presume they are also thinking they have started something they will win.

They haven't. We win the wars and battles.

Exhibit A and B, our parents. Push us too far and we will not be held responsible for our actions. Just ask the state. They said the same thing when sentencing us to Sutton.

We can't be tamed or controlled. We've tasted the crazy and the blood, and we fucking love it. It's the most free we have ever felt. I would actually consider us freed, not crazy. Free to be our-fucking-selves.

The mood stabilizers mentioned earlier, yeah, they push them down our throats, but they don't make it down ours. Since we have a private bathroom, we just vomit them up after we take them. So I guess you can say we are as stable as a fucking earthquake. Which is another reason on the long list that those cunts have not even seen a fraction of what we are capable of. They have started something they will never finish... alive.

We heard a couple of whispers that Susan left for the day shortly after we made ourselves comfortable in the TV room. Karen fucked off elsewhere. We saw her at dinner, but she only observed. Just like we observed her back. We fucking see you, Karen. You are the ringleader. Susan and Doc are under your ugly Wicked Witch of the East spell.

It's late now, well past lights out, and we are back in our room.

Everything that went down earlier only made Ris want to keep Dex closer. Tonight, he is sleeping in the spare bed we have.

Usually, he only occupies it when he has a nightmare, but considering the shit that we suspect is brewing, it's better to stay close. Ris is right for keeping him here with us. Karen and Susan better buy some shovels because they are digging their own graves. My Savage and I will gladly bury them after the three of us torture them slowly.

The thought gets my dick hard.

They will regret the day they walked through these doors. The day they thought they could test us. They will regret not keeping in fucking line like the rest of the staff here.

Fuck, enough about those two.

Savage is cuddled next to me in our bed. "He's asleep. I can tell. Wanna play with my pussy, Jasp? She has had such a long day and would love your cock to come inside of her."

Grabbing her hand, I place it on top of my already hard cock. "Do you love this cock, slut?"

"Hmm, yes. He is mine. Please let him come out

and play." Ris pouts. I can never resist her pouty lips begging for my cock.

IRIS

Today has been a strange day. I just need Jasper to make it all better.

Rubbing his cock, he has me pouting for him to come out and play. He loves making me beg for his cock. And who am I to deny him this pleasure? I will get on my knees and plead with him if I have to.

"Ok, Savage. Take him out and play. Use that filthy fucking mouth of yours," he demands.

Yummy, big bad daddy Jasper is out .

Wasting no time, I move between his spread legs on the bed and lean forward on my knees, taking in his musky smell. I'm already dripping and his cock is dying to be freed from his tight boxer briefs. Wrapping my fingers around the elastic band, I pull them down and his cock springs free. It's already dripping with precum, making my mouth water.

Sliding his underwear completely off, I throw

them to the ground as I lean down and lick the tip of his giant cock.

"Fuck, Ris. That's it. He loves when your mouth is on him."

Wrapping my lips around his head and holding his base with my hands, I move to get all of him down my throat. As I look up at him through my eyelashes, I find him looking back at me with hooded eyes.

"So fucking beautiful, take him deep, slut."

Moving my mouth up and down his shaft, I begin working him. Making sure I keep him as deep as possible. I need to feel him. Every single inch needs to be inside of me. That's when he brings his hands to my hair to keep it that way. Holding my head down so my face is flush with his body, Jasper begins to thrust into me. I don't gag. I relax my throat and let him use me. Drool begins to slide down my chin and drop onto my hands, holding the base of his cock. My eyes are watering from the lack of oxygen. I fucking love this. Let me be his fuck toy.

A small moan leaves his mouth. I look up at him, squinting to tell him that he needs to keep it down. Is he trying to wake up Dex? My Dexy does not need to see his Mama like this. It would scar my poor boy.

Jasper just smiles back at me as ropes of cum begin to

shoot out of his cock and down my throat. He continues to use me as he works himself through his orgasm, his release filling my mouth and sliding down my throat. His salty cum tastes incredible, and I am feasting on it.

My twin lets go of my hair and I slowly move my mouth up off his shaft, cleaning him and making sure not to let a drop of his cum go to waste. As I let go of his cock with my hands, I lick my lips and swallow everything.

"Such a good fucking girl. My good little slut. Let's fuck away tonight and rain hell on them tomorrow," Jasper promises.

Together, we can do anything.

"Fuck yes. They have no idea what they started. But we know how it will end. With them, dead," smiling back at him as I position myself over his cock.

I begin to slide myself down his shaft, his hard cock invading my tight, wet pussy. He fills me up perfectly.

"You feel so good," I whisper to him.

"Use me, Ris."

I plan on it.

Placing my hands on his strong chest, I ride him like it's our last day. I needed this. There is so much stress and tension built up inside of me and it needs to be released all over him.

Bouncing up and down on him, Jasper rubs that spot inside my pussy perfectly. I feel him reaching up and tightly pinch both of my nipples and it feels so fucking good. Then, throwing my head back, I start to feel a tingle move down my spine. Jasper then moves his hands from my nipples to my neck, gripping it tightly, almost cutting off my entire airway. He only leaves a little bit open so I can take the tiniest breaths while dying for more.

My orgasm hits me, my body trembles, my pussy gripping him tightly as I continue to use him, his cock rubbing against the walls of my cunt. "That's it, Savage, cum all over my cock like the filthy fucking slut you are."

That does it and I come undone. Losing all control. He lets go of my neck and I feel it hit me even harder. My eyes are rolling in the back of my head, and I'm seeing stars as my cum begins coating Jasper's cock as I continue to ride it. His cock hits all the way to my cervix. I feel so fucking full.

My pussy grips him tighter as I begin to milk him. His own release begins to empty inside of me. Ropes of his cum coat the inside of my pussy. It's the best fucking feeling. No two people can be as close as we are now or ever. He holds my hips down as he uses me, thrusting into me a couple more times until his own orgasm dies down.

Sweat is dripping down my forehead as mine starts to fade. As I try to catch my breath, I lean forward with him still inside of me and rest my head on his sweaty chest. It's moving rapidly under me, and I can hear his heart beating. It's so soothing.

As I look up at him, I catch him looking down at me. His eyes say everything. This man loves me. And I fucking love him.

We lay like this for a while before speaking up, "Jasp, can I ask you something?"

Jasper is rubbing my head. "Always, Savage."

"I want you to tattoo me. Will you?"

"Really? I would fucking love to. What are you thinking?" He whispers with excitement.

Now sitting up on him, I lift my head up to expose more of my neck and explain what I want. "Yours. Across my neck."

He grabs my face with his strong hands, angling me so I am looking back at him, and he crashes his lips into mine. Jasp pulls back slightly while looking into my eyes. "Stay here. I'll get my stuff."

Our cum is leaking out of me as I roll off Jasp and sit up against my headboard on my side of the bed and wait. Jasper jumps off the bed, still naked, and rushes to where our dresser is. He kneels down and begins to shimmy a piece of the wood flooring up. He has to hide his tools. They would be confiscated if they were ever found. It's so stupid.

Once he has everything, Jasp rushes back over and flicks on the small bedside lamp. "Ok, Savage. Lay back, rest your head on the pillow. It will hurt and it will take a while only having this paperclip, but it will look so fucking sexy on your neck, I promise."

"I trust you, Jasp. Let's do this," smiling back at him as I lay my head down like he told me.

The only other person he has used this stuff on has been himself, so I don't mind him not sanitizing it. It's not like we have anything to use other than the soap and water, anyway.

He wastes no time straddling my lap as I lay down on the pillow like he instructed.

It makes this moment even more intimate.

"This is our vow to each other, yours and mine. We are fucking one, Savage. I own you as much as you own me," he whispers, and he begins to poke my neck with the sharp tool.

"I love you, Jasp."

"I love you too, Savage."

I lay completely still, not wanting to mess

anything up. It stings a little. The neck has thinner skin, so it is a more sensitive place. But it is all worth it. I close my eyes so I can focus on how it feels; deprived of my sight, the feeling only intensifies. I love the pain when Jasper is the one inflicting it. It's beautiful. He does it with such love and possessiveness. I crave it. I crave him.

Hearing the tiny pokes into my skin. It cracks ever so slightly. After every couple, he takes the black ink from the pen and puts it onto his finger. He rubs it over what he has just completed, gently. It's sexual and intimate. It's making my pussy wet again.

No Iris. You must focus. Sex after. First, our vow.

"I can smell you from here, Ris. Don't worry, I'll eat your sweet pussy once I'm done."

His whispered words cause me to bite my lip in anticipation. My brother can eat pussy like no other. I have never had another man there. I would never. But I imagine my brother is the best in the game, at all of it.

Thank fuck, Dex is a heavy sleeper because I need my brother's lips on mine as soon as fucking possible.

I lay here for the next forty-five minutes, letting Jasper do his magic. I know he is making sure it's perfect.

"Ok. It's done."

I open my eyes and see him admiring his work. He is so beautiful.

Breaking his trance, I whisper. "Can I see it?"

Jasper gets off of me and grabs my hand. We both make our way off the bed and into our bathroom. He flicks the light on and positions me in front of the mirror, and it's incredible.

In capital letters, he placed YOURS where my neck meets my jaw bone. Exactly where his MINE would land when he chokes me during sex. Where he squeezes the life almost out of me, but with raw fucking passion behind it. He even added a few wisps off the letters to make it more feminine.

Tears prickle my eyes. I want to touch it but know I can't until it's healed, "It's beautiful, Jasp. Perfect. Thank you so much."

"Of course, Ris. I wish I could have done it better, but it's the best I could do with what I have." He says, shrugging his shoulders.

Spinning around, I grab his face with my hands and tilt his head down so he is looking at me. "I promise, I love it. I wouldn't want it any other way."

"Good. Now. Let me eat that wet pussy."

JASPER

Last night was fucking something else. I didn't expect Savage to want me to mark her. I've been dying to. But I wanted it to be her decision.

Being able to take my needle to her delicate skin. Watching droplets of blood run down her neck while I rubbed in the ink. It's an image I've had on repeat in my mind ever since. I hope she wants more. I need to mark every inch of her with me.

I'm fucking thankful Dex didn't wake during any of that. If he did, he hasn't alluded to it. But I think Ris would be more traumatized knowing he'd caught us than he would be.

After I gave Ris her tattoo, I ate her pussy like my life depended on it. It kind of did. I needed to taste her after solidifying our vows for every single fucking person in here to see.

Mine and yours.

We have always been one before we were even born. We are blood. We will never be divided.

It's almost like it symbolizes a new chapter for us. Because going into today, it's the start of something big. Something that once we pass go, it cannot be taken back. Those fuckers think they can fuck with us? We will fuck with them ten times over. We are the Queen and King of Sutton. They are about to be reminded of it.

"Ris, are you almost ready?" I grumble from the bed. I've been dressed for twenty minutes already. So has Dex. He is sitting on the edge of the spare bed waiting in his black jeans, black t-shirt, and red and black Air Jordan's. I'm in similar attire. My black jeans are distressed and I have a black baggy tee with matching Jordans. Ris pleaded with us to be all matchy. After some push back we agreed. We would have done it without moaning, but we can't let her think she holds all the power over us, even though she does. But shit, I can only imagine what she's got planned.

"Almost!" Ris shouts from the bathroom.

Staring up at the ceiling, "Dex. We gotta stick

together. Whatever happens in the dining hall, it will set the fucking tone. It declares war on these bitches. And this place by default. We gotta get rid of them and protect our own. You should have seen it yesterday in session, Doc is captured in their spell. They hold some fucking power over him. It was clear as fucking day, painted all over his ugly mug."

I don't need to look at him to know he gets it and agrees.

That's when Ris jumps out of the bathroom declaring cheerfully, "Boys! I'm ready!"

Sitting up from the bed, I see her rushing over to Dex and jumping on his lap. Ris snuggles close to him and whispers something I can't hear into his ear.

It doesn't make me jealous. I know they have something special and that it's completely platonic.

But fuck does she look stunning straddling him, her delicate face now resting on his shoulder. Her long black hair is slicked back in a high pony. Dark eye makeup with a bright red lip. She's wearing a distressed black crop tank, black high-waisted bike shorts and Jordans that match ours.

Ris looks over to me, smiling, mischief dancing in her eyes.

Taking a better look at her, I notice she also has drawn two black tear drops by the corner of her eyes.

Fuck me, this girl shows no mercy.

She's sending a message. Tear drops are for the fallen. Two of them are drawn on her, one for both Karen and Susan. My girl is amazing.

"Hey, lift your chin up, show Dex." I tell her.

She does exactly what I instruct without hesitating. Dex just looks at it for a moment, then goes to touch it out of curiosity, but he stops himself before she does.

"That's right, Dexy. We can't touch it until it's healed. But isn't it beautiful?" Ris coos at him.

Dex nods, still examining it. A smile forms on his face as he brings his Mama in for another snuggle.

"Dex. If you ever want anything done. Just let me know, man, I got you."

He looks at me, acknowledging what I said.

Ris pulls back from the hug. "My boys, you both look so handsome! And look! We match. This is going to be so much fun!" Giggling as she jumps off Dex and heads toward me, holding her hand out. I grab it, standing up as she leads us out of the room.

"You look perfect, Savage," whispering into her ear.

Looking back at me with her sinister smile, "Today is going to be a great day boys!"

The three of us make it down to breakfast and grab our food. Breakfast today consists of toast, fruit, and oatmeal. Same bland shit as every other day. At least it's better than prison food. I heard you can't even tell what it is you're actually eating in prison. So I guess we can consider ourselves lucky, if that's what you want to call it.

We woke up earlier than normal this morning. We wanted to make sure we got here first thing when it was the busiest. We are going to light this fucking place up and want the biggest audience possible.

I've finished eating, so now I wait, sitting back on the chair, watching Ris and Dex finish their meals. We didn't go over a plan. We don't do organized shit well, unless we absolutely have to. Taking these bitches out and getting Sutton back to the way it was before they came is the end-game. We don't need punishments or structure or proper treatment. We are never getting out of here. None of that will do us any good. We will never learn. This is us.

I'm still racking my brain over it. Don't they know we are fucking crazy and some of us are even killers? It's why we are all here, and they want to test us? They want to challenge our authority in our home? It makes no fucking sense. But there is no denying it, they have balls.

I hear Ris clear her throat, which brings me back from my thoughts.

Both her and Dex have finished eating. She looks at both of us and smiles, which means it's fucking go time.

Ris stands up, adjusts her shirt and checks the rest of herself out before stepping onto her chair. She holds both her hands out, and Dex and I stand to grab onto one each as she takes more steps to stand on the table. Letting go of her, all I can think is, fuck, she's going big.

Both of us stand back to watch the Queen make the magic happen.

"Hello! Excuse me. I am so sorry to interrupt your incredible breakfast, but I have a few announcements to make," Ris yells into the room. She waits until everyone is looking at her before continuing.

"Firstly, thank you all for being here this morning. Ms. O, you are looking fresh as always!"

Ms. O is one of the older residents. She's short, maybe five feet tall on a good day, a short mom hair cut with white hair, wire-framed glasses and she likes to keep it casual with runners, shorts and a t-shirt most days. Don't let her appearance fool you, though.

She's absolutely batshit crazy. Rumor has it that over twenty years ago, she caught her husband cheating. Killed him and the chick. Dismembered them, shoved her husband's fist up the chick's ass. Then cut his dick off and shoved it up his own ass and his balls were pinned to the chick's chest. When they found them, she was covered in blood and laughing hysterically, admiring her work. Since being here, they keep her pretty medicated, but she still has her moments. She will attack other female residents that annoy her. Cackle at absolutely nothing. A typical day here, really. So, naturally, Savage became obsessed with Ms.O.

"Secondly, the Grey's finale is in a couple days. We will be having a watch party in the TV room. Bring snacks! And! No fuck ups this year… Susan!" she glares and points her finger towards Susan, who has just walked in with Karen right behind her. Right on time.

"Next. It is Mr.H's birthday next week. Don't forget! Make sure you stop by his room to wish him well. He absolutely loves his birthday, so let's make it special, people!"

It's not his birthday. Every couple months he decides it is because he likes the attention and I fuck Ris up the ass for him on special occasions in the hall.

We go along with it. It makes him happy. Who are we to take away someone's happiness?

"Lastly. Karen and Susan. I'm so pleased, our guests of honor are here today! Thank you for joining us."

Before she can finish, Karen starts walking toward us and shouts at Ris,

"Get off the table. Now." This bitch will never learn. She has no authority here.

Ris smiles at Karen before continuing, "I was in the middle of speaking, do you mind? You don't tell me or anyone else here what to do!" Savage screeches.

"I'll call the doctor. You know what will happen if he has to come here," Karen threatens.

I decide to jump in, before Ris completely loses it. "Do it, Karen. I dare you. Show everyone you're incapable of handling anything yourself. Show your incompetence when all she is doing is giving the people morning announcements. Call him. Or step the fuck back. Now."

Karen doesn't say anything, nor does she move.

Ris wastes no time in starting up again. "Thank you Jasper. As I was saying. We haven't properly welcomed Karen and Susan to Sutton yet, have we? Let's give them a warm welcome and make sure to continue it throughout the day! I really want them to feel special."

Then my beautiful Savage brings the chaos and starts cheering and jumping on the table. Clapping her hands and encouraging the others to join her.

They do. The other residents start cackling and pounding their fists into their tables. Some even fist pump into the air.

Dex and I join in. I blow a few loud whistles. But we aren't cheering for Karen and Susan. We are cheering our girl on. Before you know it, a bunch of aides rush the room. They must have heard the commotion. I notice one goes towards Ms.O, who is on her feet; he pulls out a syringe, most likely a sedative, but he doesn't stand a chance. She starts barking at him and showing off her teeth.

Haha, let the chaos begin mother fuckers.

7

IRIS

This is amazing! It's pure madness in here and I did it.

Me!

With the help of my boys, of course.

But this image in front of me is a dream. Seeing Ms.O trying to bite one aide makes me love her spirit even more. A few other residents decide to have the aides chase them around the room for fun. Everyone is having a great time. I do notice Susan is inconveniently missing. The doctor will be here any minute. There's nowhere else she would have gone. Fucking narc. Snitches get stitches, Susan.

Karen is still in front of us, my brother and Dex making a barrier made of muscle between her and I.

It takes every bone in my body to resist the urge to jump on her and pound her face beyond recognition. To be covered in all her crimson blood that would be gushing out of her mouth and nose as I continue to beat her precious little face in. The thought alone is orgasmic. I dream of the day I can take my thumbs and push them into her beady little eyes.

Karen is fucking mine. It's decided. When the time comes, I will destroy this bitch.

We are staring each other down while I'm still standing on the table. Our eyes are locked, neither of us budging.

"Iris Ashford! Get off the table, NOW!" Doctor Peters has arrived. I love when he gets all shouty at me. It actually turns me on. The dominance, the aggression… Oh Henry, if you only knew. Obviously, it's nothing compared to Jasper, but a girl can have a crush, can't she?

"As you wish, Doctor Peters," I say sweetly, smiling back at him. Susan is standing like the coward she is behind him. I grab hold of my boy's shoulders and jump off the table. The rest of the room has gone still and silent.

Ms. O is putting away her teeth, and the game of tag has stopped. They are all waiting to see what happens next. My money is on the basement for me. Standing between the boys, I don't say a word, waiting for Doc to take the lead. I am not going to suggest the basement until he does.

Henry's face is red. His chest is heaving with heavy breaths under his black polo shirt.

He pinches the bridge of his nose. "Iris. Jasper. Dex. Your rooms, now! Stay there until I decide what to fucking do with you three. No leaving them. Your doors stay open, and there's no talking to anyone who walks by. Someone will bring you food at mealtime. The rest of you sit down and finish your breakfast! And outside time is canceled for the next two days. I hope it was worth it!"

I grab both the boy's hands and start to lead us out of the room, but Karen refuses to move as we approach her. "Move, Karen. You heard Henry. We have our rooms to get to."

She still stands in place for a moment before conceding and stepping aside. That's right, bitch.

As we approach Doctor Peters, I keep my head held high. "Don't worry Henry, we will be on our best behavior," adding a wink as we pass. I swear if his head could explode, that is what would have done it. I feel proud knowing that. That I have this effect on him that no one else does.

Finally, we pass the narc, Susan. She will get hers too.

"Iris, Dex goes to his room. Not yours," the good Doctor adds just as we are about to exit the room. Fuck.

I squeeze both Dex and Jasper's hands, as a hint to not react. They want us to react. We cannot fall for it. We achieved a lot this morning and we cannot ruin it.

Together, we walk away, continuing toward the stairs without a response. Dex's room is next to ours, but it's still too far away. I need him with us, and he needs to be with his Mama.

"It will be ok, Ris. If anyone tries to get to him, they have to pass by our room first. We will see and I will fucking stop them," Jasper whispers into my ear. He knows I'm panicking internally about the Doctor's orders. I nod my head in response.

Dex must have heard Jasp because he squeezes my hand tightly to reassure me. I know he is strong. He can take care of himself, but I don't like this. My mind is racing as we walk up the stairs and make it into the hall where our rooms are. I break the silence. "Why aren't I being taken to the basement?"

"I don't know. Maybe they know it won't work on you because it never does. Maybe they figure you being out and not able to see Dex will punish you more than being in the basement? I can only guess."

Jasper is right, being out and having a wall between Dex and us does kill me.

"Maybe you're right."

We pass Mr. H's room, but he doesn't poke his head out. Shame really, I need to tell him his special show may be on hold if the good doctor has his way. We reach mine and Jasper's doorway, "Dex, if you need anything, you bang on your wall. I will hear it and I'll bang back to let you know I'm there. Ok, big guy?"

He lets go of my hand and brings me in for a hug. He smells of his musky deodorant. I whisper against his chest, "Love you, Dexy, always."

Dex kisses the top of my head, gives me one final squeeze and releases me. He makes eye contact with Jasper, then turns around to walk to his room. I stay in the hall watching him until he makes his way in and I can no longer see him.

Fucking bastards.

Maybe Jasper is right—this is far worse than the basement. I refuse to let it show that they have gotten to me. They will only see it as a weakness and use it against me further. I am positive they have a camera in the hall. The way Doc says he sees everything at our session almost confirmed it.

Not knowing where it is, I lift my middle fingers

up and do a complete circle while staying in place to make sure he sees this, too.

Jasper starts laughing at me as I start on my second spin of the room. "Savage, I think he gets it. Fuck him and those two bitches. Now, let me help take your mind off this morning."

I stop in place, "Oh, yes please!" Rushing into the room where Jasper is already standing, he has already removed his shirt and fuck me, what a fine specimen he is. His six-pack is on display as I move my eyes up his body. He is beautiful with those dimples on his cheeks, his deep brown eyes and dark shaggy hair hanging over his forehead. Walking toward him, I reach my hand up as I break our distance and rake my fingers through his hair, his eyes never leaving me.

Standing on my tippy toes, I whisper into his ear, "Don't be gentle."

JASPER

The moment I hear those three beautiful words leave my Savage's mouth, my hand is around her throat. Just below where I marked her last night. Her inked 'yours' fits perfectly with the 'mine' on my hand. Our lips lock, and she parts them, allowing my tongue to enter her sweet mouth. I start moving her backward toward the wall until I hear her back connect with it, then squeeze her throat a bit harder. I want it to leave a mark. I want to see my thumb prints on her skin. Our lips still connected, I bring the kiss even deeper as I feel her throat in my hand contracting faster in my grasp. The sound of Ris gasping for air hardens my already hard cock. I am her only source of oxygen now. I fucking love having this power. I don't take it for granted. She owns me, and I know she can take it away from me at any time.

I feel her fingertips brush against my chest, causing me to shiver. That's when I pull back slightly and whisper against her lips, "On your knees."

Letting go of her throat, I tilt her face up to mine and watch as she inhales a deep breath into her lungs. I see tears streaming down her cheeks where her makeup has smudged. She is so fucking beautiful. Ris lowers herself to her knees as I instructed, her eyes not leaving mine the whole way down.

She looks up at me through her eyelashes, waiting for my next instruction. I undo the button of my jeans, then unzip them. Pushing them and my underwear to my feet, stepping out of them, leaving me fully naked. My hard cock is on full display for her.

Ris bites her lip, staring at it and I know she's itching to touch me, but I keep her waiting. I know this is torture for her and she's likely dripping at the thought of it. Gripping my cock with my hand, I pump myself a couple times, making her watch as precum begins to drip from the tip.

"Take your shorts and panties off and turn around, stay on your knees, and put both your hands against the fucking wall."

She listens, quickly undoing her shorts and shimmying out of them and her lace panties, kicking them toward our bed. Keeping her shirt and shoes on, Ris turns like I told her and braces herself against the wall.

"I can smell your pussy from here," I tell her.

Lowering myself to my knees, I spit in my hand to use it as lube on my cock. Lining myself with her perfect ass, I begin slowly pushing myself into her. Ris moans against the wall as I continue to inch myself inside her ass. No matter how often I fuck her here, it's always so tight for me. I am half-way in when I grip both her hips tight with my hands while I continue to make my way inside of her.

"Jasper, don't be gentle. I can take it. Please," Ris pleads.

She has no idea. This is the only gentleness she will see from me today. I slowly inch further until I'm fully inside of her, pausing for a moment to allow her to adjust to the intrusion.

Checking in with her one last time, "Are you ready, Savage?"

Nodding her head back, "Yes. Do it."

I pull myself almost all the way out before slamming back into her with everything I have.

Ris screams fill the room, "Ah, fuck. That's it, brother. Fucking get lost with me. Fuck my ass as hard as you can!"

Squeezing her hips with my hands, I need to leave my marks on her here, too. I need to leave them all over her. I am obsessed with my girl. I keep this pace with her, thrusting myself into her without mercy. Thrusting as hard as I fucking can and each time I slam back in her, she throws her head back while making the most beautiful noises. She loves it rough. She gets off on it as much as I do, if not more. I reach one hand forward and take one of her nipples between my thumb and forefinger, pinching it as hard as I can. At the same time, I move back into her, and it's the hardest one yet. My pelvis connects with her ass, and she clenches around my cock harder. I won't last much longer. She's making herself even tighter around me. I love how her body reacts to me.

"That's it Savage, such a good fucking girl for me. You. are. Mine!"

"Yours! Yours, Jasp, keep going. Please keep going." She's panting hard now.

Moving my hand from her nipple, I place it back around her throat and squeeze. I move quicker now, chasing my own release. I can feel my back start to tingle as I thrust faster and faster inside of her ass.

As I am about to cum, I feel her body begin to tremble as her own orgasm hits. I hear her trying to gasp for the air that I won't let enter her. Her chest is heaving, her lungs violently contracting. All of this only adds to the experience, intensifying it. Once I feel like she might be on the verge of blacking out, I let go of her throat. Her orgasm is still riding through her and now she's gasping desperately for the air she needs. It is sensory overload for her and I fucking love that I am the one who has done this to her.

She moans louder now as I reach forward between her creamy white thighs to play with her clit and work her through it all.

"That's it Savage, keep gripping me tight," I praise

her, as my cock swells and I start cumming deep inside of her. I work myself in her ass, rapidly slamming myself into her. Ropes of cum coat her insides as she milks me.

Her own release begins to subside while I continue working myself through mine. I slam into her a couple more times before stopping and collapsing on her, resting my sweaty head on her back.

Still panting, she breathes out, "I hope you left marks."

This gives me an idea. I slowly pull out of her so I can watch my cum drip out of her beautiful hole. Bringing my mouth forward towards her hole, I lick some of what is leaking out. Then, leaning back on the heels of my feet, I bring my hand back and slap it against her ass cheek with full force. As it connects, you can hear the skin crack, and it causes my own hand to tingle. Ris yelps loudly, still braced against the wall.

"If the others didn't leave my mark on you, this one will."

Ris turns her head toward me, and there's a sinister smile on her face. This girl is completely fucked up, and I crave her crazy.

I pull her hips back against my body, and our

mouths connect. We devour each other until we hear a whistle. Then another one. What the fuck?

Our lips part, "Hmm, you taste good, Jasp." Ris tells me.

Another whistle breaks the silence, and I stand up with Ris still in my hold. Placing her on the bed, I walk naked to our door, which is still open as per Doc's orders.

Poking my head out to the hall, I see Mr.H.

"You did well, my boy. Excellent performance. I could hear you both from here."

Shaking my head, I take a deep breath, "Thank you, yeah, I'm glad you enjoyed it."

"Yes, I just needed to commend you both. I will leave you both back to it, then."

Mr.H's head leaves his frame and disappears back into his room.

I turn around and face Ris, who is now laughing hysterically on the bed.

"That's enough out of you, Savage. Go clean yourself up and get changed. Who knows when those fuckheads will decide to come up here and check on us."

Still laughing as she sits up and scurries up to me, "Sir, yes, sir! As you command," then kisses my nose.

It makes me smile, which then causes her to poke both my dimples before running off to our bathroom.

"I'll make your other cheek red too if you don't behave," I shout back at her.

Ris pokes her head out of the bathroom door taunting me, "Don't threaten me with a good time now, brother," before going back in and closing the door behind her.

I fucking love that girl.

This was a good distraction for both of us. There's something brewing, and we needed this before the chaos really kicks off.

IRIS

They had us held up in our rooms all fucking day yesterday. After I cleaned myself off from the fantastic ass pounding my brother gave me, I had a nap out of boredom.

Hours later, Jasper woke me with food that the aides had left. He said he tried to get information out of them. Asking how much longer and if I would get a harsher punishment, but they refused to speak to him. Just passed the food over and left.

Bastards.

Although, it was lasagna night! So that made me happy. I just love it. I think it has to be one of my favorite foods. But they did hold back the garlic bread. If it wasn't war before, this definitely declared it!

Shortly after eating, Jasper mentioned he had

thought of a plan for our next session. I begged to know what it was. Even tried to bribe him with an epic blow job, but the boy didn't budge. He said he needed me to respond 'naturally' to what he had planned, which made me even more excited. Who doesn't love a surprise from the one they love?

He really does spoil me.

After that, I went and sat by the wall that separated Dex and us. Knocking on it a couple of times before I heard Dex knock back. I hated that he was alone in there. He should be with me. I am his Mama. How dare they separate us.

I needed to comfort him, so I decided to tell him a quick bedtime story. Well, it was more a threat to any bad dream that dared enter his room and mind. I talked about how I would slaughter all the monsters that try to invade his dreams. How he will always be protected and safe. And happy. I always want him to be happy. He knocked back twice after, and I did two back and told him I loved him before moving back to the bed with Jasper.

This morning they brought us breakfast, late. I think that was on fucking purpose. The aide told us we had twenty minutes to eat before we were due in Doctor Peters' office.

Thankfully, we were already dressed, otherwise

he could have shoved the twenty minute warning up his ass. And I would have gladly shoved it there.

Now, we are sitting in Henry's office. The three of us on the same couch. He has had us waiting for what feels like ages. Why demand us to be down here and then be nowhere to be found when we arrive?

It's bad manners.

My irritated thought is broken by the sound of his office door opening. Henry walks through it, still looking very angry. He's wearing a blue polo shirt today. It really brings out his eyes. He doesn't say a word while walking over to his chair that's across from us. As Doctor Peters sits down, he lets out a large and very dramatic sigh. "You three have crossed the line. Yesterday was a display of complete and utter disrespect towards me, the other staff and patients."

"Residents, we are residents!" I refuse to have any of us identified as patients. It has always bothered me. We are alleged to be 'unsafe and crazy' individuals who cannot be treated and released. We are never getting out of here. We are residents.

"Enough!"

Shit, we are in for a lecture of a lifetime now.

"Iris, your behavior yesterday was completely out

of line. Causing a riot at breakfast! What point are you three trying to prove?"

Me? Out of hand? Never.

"Henry. I was just giving the people Sutton's morning announcements. If anyone caused anything, it was Karen. That bitch is out of control. I've told you this before. She needs a program. Not me!"

"You need to get over your dislike towards her and Beth…"

I don't let him finish. "Susan. Her name is Susan now."

"Regardless, they aren't going anywhere!" the Doctor declares, as he slams his fist into the armrests of his chair.

Oops!

"You know Doc. You have a point. Maybe we can use today's session for something beneficial to all of us?" Jasper says, leaning forward with his elbows resting on his knees. "Couples therapy."

What does he mean by couples therapy? We don't need therapy, I turn to look at him. "Jasp, we don't need therapy!"

"Ris, Savage, hear me out. Doc, what do you say?"

Doctor Peters rolls his eyes at Jasper. Well, that was rude!

"I can't believe I'm agreeing to this. Fine, Jasper. I'll humor you."

Jasper blows out a breath before continuing. "You see Doc, I know Ris has a crush on you. I'm fine with it, really. But I know she dreams of having both of us fuck her at the same time. The thing is, you aren't getting anywhere near my pussy, so you would have to take her ass. I also don't want my dick within an arm's reach of yours, Doc. It's nothing personal, just how I feel. I like my Savage all to myself. So I think I've come up with a compromise, and I hope you could help guide us through this."

What in the holy fuck is happening? Could my dreams be coming true today? This has to be the big surprise Jasp had planned for me. The man is a romantic.

"Jasper. You are completely delusional if you think I'm falling for this nonsense. She's my patient. It's unethical, completely immoral, and irresponsible!"

"So, it's not completely out of the question, then? I was thinking, what if I just watch from here while you fuck her ass?"

I don't mind that compromise. It's actually really thoughtful.

Doctor Peters stands up and starts shouting,

"Absolutely not. This entire thing will never be in the realm of possibilities. This is a prime example of why you're both in my care. You both are completely delusional to reality!"

"Sit. The. Fuck. Down. Doc!" Jasper stands and matches his tone. It doesn't take long for Dex to follow, and he's on his feet almost instantly.

"You three do not intimidate me. Or the Nurses. You will learn quickly that things are going to be different around here. We are going to talk about what led the three of you to be here, under my care. Under the state's care."

Quicker than I can even register. Dex moves forward, moving behind Doctor Peter's chair, putting his hands on Henry's shoulders and pushes him back down into his chair.

Jasper gets right in his face. "Savage, come here beautiful."

Oh, this is getting exciting!

I stand up and walk over to my brother.

"Yes, brother?"

"Touch the good Doc, Ris. I think we will find he will show how he really feels better this way. Isn't that right Doc? Sometimes we aren't always able to verbalize how we feel. Sometimes we show it? Isn't that what you said once?"

"Dex. Let. Me. Go. This won't end well for you, son"

Oh no, he fucking didn't. I see red.

"Did you just threaten him? You will not touch a hair on his fucking head! I will end you if you even try. Do you understand, Henry? And he is NOT. YOUR. SON!" Now I'm mad. This could have been a great time amongst friends, but Henry had to go and goddamn ruin it!

I take my hand and place it on his pants, directly on top of his soft, small dick, and start rubbing. I can feel it start to get hard under my touch. Oh Henry, you do want this after all.

Sadly, due to his vile attitude towards Dex, our once beautiful love affair is officially over. This is all just a game now. And I fucking love games.

"That's it, Savage. Get the good Doc nice and hard. He fucking loves this, don't you, Doc? Ris touching your cock like this. Must feel much better than when Karen or Susan does it."

Henry's face slacks

"Yeah, we know." Jasper starts laughing in his face. And even if we didn't. This confirms it. Doctor Peters really has been a naughty boy.

Without breaking eye contact with Doc, "Savage, be a good fucking girl for me. Come sit on

Doc's lap for me. Rub your needy pussy on his small cock."

I remove my hand and begin to replace it with my body. Moving in front of Jasper, I place a knee on either side of Henry's legs and straddle him. I grind myself against him a few times, and it doesn't take long before his eyes become hooded and his breaths quicken. I'm betting he could cum at any moment. But before we can allow that, I lean into him. He has to know this isn't him being rewarded for bad behavior. This is a warning.

Placing my lips against his ear, I smile and whisper, "Don't make me hurt you. It would be wise not to challenge us, Henry."

It's not a threat. It's a fucking promise. This is our house, our home. We will make it rain hell fire in this place if we have to.

9

JASPER

Ris is straddling Doc. Dex is holding him down. I get right into his face. He wanted to treat us. He basically set this up for us on a silver platter.

"You want to know why we did it? You want to talk about why I killed my mother, Doc? Why Ris, my beautiful Savage, my fucking queen, killed our father? You want to extract these demons from us and suddenly we become upstanding citizens? Who's the delusional one now, Doc? It will never work. We are how we are. But since you asked so nicely, I'll tell you why."

"They had Ris half naked and tied to the fucking kitchen table. They had me tied to a chair. Forced to watch what he was going to do. He was going to fucking touch her! She is mine to touch, not his! Mother stood by and let it happen. That brainless fucking cunt did nothing! She never did anything to help us! They both got what they deserved. My only regrets are getting caught and not taking the time to torture them longer! The only good thing about this place is I get to fuck that sweet pussy whenever I want. And that she found Dex. We are a family. You don't just fuck with one of us. We all feel it."

It's silent. My chest is heaving. My face is red. All I see is red. The memory of that day. The best and worst day of our lives. Ris covered in blood. She was fucking gorgeous. I shake my head to rid it of her beautiful image. I need to focus.

"Does that answer your question, Doc?" I spit at him.

He doesn't respond.

Ris grabs his face and slaps him. You can hear the crack as soon as her hand connects to his cheek. "He asked you a question!"

I know she can feel the rage inside of me.

Doc's eyes widen from the shock of the slap.

"You three are so fucked. I will not allow you to get away with the stunt from yesterday and now this. You have crossed the line. I wanted to help you. But this has gone too fucking far! Now get your goddamn hands off me!" Doc fires back at us.

I look at Dex and nod. He lets go of Doc's shoulders and takes a step back.

I grab Ris by her hair, forcing her head back, and kiss her. Electricity shoots through me. It's always raw passion with us. Pulling back, I look at her. And I can tell by the look in her eyes that she knows what's next. They look disappointed, but we have to play the long game with this, "But Jasper, he hasn't even cum yet," she pouts.

"I know, and you will get your opportunity with him again. I promise."

Either fucking him or killing him. She will have her moment, regardless.

Ris gives him one last rub before fully removing herself from his lap. Getting up, she stands in front of me. My front to her back, I reach up and grab her throat with my hand, holding her close. The word 'mine' is visible to the good doctor.

"Don't think I didn't notice the ink on her neck, Jasper. We will find your tools. Mark my words."

"You do that, Doc." He won't find shit. They have looked before and they can look again. They won't find it. If they do, I will just make new ones.

"Don't say I didn't warn you three. If you had complied with the treatment, everything coming to you could have been avoided. Do you get that? It didn't have to be this way,"

Ris speaks up, "We have never had an issue until you allowed those two to come in and act like they run us. We run us. Not them!"

Doc shakes his head. "They are trying to provide better structure. Hold people accountable so the inmates don't run the asylum. You are the inmates. You are the patients. But I don't need to explain myself or these decisions to you. I set the rules. You three follow them! Now, go to your rooms. Dex, you to yours. Your consequences are coming."

I roll my eyes at his dramatics, removing my hand from Ris's neck and move it to hold her hand. She reaches her other hand to Dex, and he grabs it immediately. For those two to be separated multiple days in a row isn't good. She's going to be furious and Dex anxious.

"I don't want to cause even more of an uproar, but thanks to your outburst yesterday, other patients are now on edge. I will let you three walk back to your rooms without an escort. But know that I'll see if you don't obey my instruction."

We don't respond to his threats.

Instead, we leave his office, walk down the long hall toward the grand staircase and make our way back up to our floor and rooms. We don't make eye contact with anyone, we also don't show any expression on our faces. He is right. The others look to us for guidance and we can't let it show that we are rattled by anything... yet.

Once we make it in front of our doors, we all let out a long sigh.

"Dexy, remember. Knock on the wall if you need me. I will do the same. They can't keep us banished to our rooms for long. People will start wondering what's going on if all three of us are missing. Plus, we deserve some outside time. We have rights too, ya know."

Watching Savage say goodbye to Dex again kills me. I know she is trying to make light of the situation. Even I know that after our session just now, we won't be getting anything good from this place for a while.

Ris wraps her arms around Dex's neck. "I love you, Dexy."

He nuzzles his head into her neck and you can faintly hear him whisper back, "Mama."

"Dex, you need anything you knock on that wall. I

will be over in a heartbeat," Dex looks up at me and nods. That's all I need. He knows we are family.

I walk into our room first, leaving Ris and Dex to have a moment alone. It isn't long after when she comes in.

"Come here Savage," I say, holding my hand out, sitting on our bed.

She walks over and lays next to me, placing her head on my lap. My sweet Savage.

I watch her as I rub her hair. She is so fucking beautiful even when she's sad, but I also know this will pass once we are all reunited after whatever punishment they have in store for us.

Lost in my thoughts, I don't even notice our door has been slammed shut until I hear it slam against the frame, then the click of the lock. The locks are on the outside here. So we cannot lock ourselves in, allegedly for our own safety.

Then we hear a blood-curdling scream. It's Dex.

Ris is up and at the door within seconds, trying to open the door. I am right behind her.

"Ris, Savage, move. I'm going to try and knock it down."

She doesn't respond back, just moves. Her eyes are a mix of rage and turmoil.

I begin ramming my shoulder against the hard wooden door, hoping to knock it down. I have to. We need to get to Dex.

"You mother fucking cocksuckers let us out," she screams.

I try charging the door a couple more times. It's not budging.

Ris starts to bang on it. Pulling the handle. Anything to try and get to him.

"Give me the needle. We need to sedate him." We can hear Karen through the door.

"DON'T. TOUCH. HIM. YOU BITCH!" Ris roars.

I grab the handle now, moving her hand out of the way, and begin yanking on it as hard as I fucking can. Fuck! We have to get to Dex!

We hear things crashing to the floor outside. Fuck yes, come on buddy, keep fighting.

"Jasper. Please do something!" Savage is frantic.

"I'm trying. This door is too solid for me to get through."

My shoulder is starting to feel the effects of it.

Ris keeps banging against the wood door and I start to pull on the handle.

We hear Dex crying, "Mama! Mama! Mama!"

My eyes widened. Why won't this door open!

Karen snarks back, "You stupid boy, your Mama isn't coming for you. She doesn't love you. She only uses you, just like she uses her brother. That girl is nothing more than a manipulative bitch. She. Doesn't. Want. You! If she did, she would be here fighting for you, but she isn't! She isn't coming!"

"Mama!" Dex shouts again in agony. Then I hear what sounds like a fist going through a wall. How is this happening?

"Dexy, don't listen to her. I love you. Mama fucking loves you! I'm coming, don't give up. Fight back. Dexy, fight!" Ris screams through the door.

"Keep him still, damnit!" Karen shouts, to whom I presume are the aides helping her.

"Mama... Mama!"

"That's it, hold him. I only brought one needle with me."

Fuck, Fuck, Fuck. We need to get to him.

I keep trying to get through the door. It's not budging, but I will not give up. I can't give up.

But, as each second goes by, the crashing and banging lessens.

I don't hear him anymore.

My heart is racing. We failed him.

I look down at Ris, and I can see tears pooling in her eyes.

"Dexy, I'm coming! Mama is coming," Ris pleads through the door ,sounding defeated and absolutely fucking destroyed.

Then. It's silent.

We both stand still. What will come next?

Then we hear something sliding against the wood floors, moving past our door then down the hall. The sound grows quieter as it gets further away. They are dragging him. How fucking dare they drag him!

Pounding my fists against the door, "You bastards! You fucking bastards! He didn't do anything. Take me. Leave him alone!"

Ris starts to scream at the top of her lungs, her nails scratching along the door as her body begins to fall to the ground.

Tears now running down her cheeks, her mascara running down alongside them.

By hurting him, they have hurt her. Which in turn hurts me. I hate seeing her like this.

I crouch down next to her, my beautiful Savage, and pick her up into my arms and place her in my lap, holding her tightly against me.

"Shh, Savage, it's going to be ok. We will make

the fuckers pay. I promise. Just like we made mother and father pay." I reassure her.

Another scream leaves her trembling body.

"Ris, I know. I got you. We will get him back, I promise. I fucking promise."

She doesn't respond. Instead, she snuggles in closer to me. They have fucking broken my Savage. I will break them for this.

10

IRIS

It's damp, cold and dark.

Cold cement bricks line the room, a steel door with thick metal bars on the top half is in the center of the wall.

The basement and I are old friends.

Doc sends me down here at least three times a year for inappropriate behavior. Which is complete bullshit. My behavior is only inappropriate to him because I just finished breaking a couple of his fingers.

Don't put your fingers in my face if you don't want them broken. Seems pretty obvious. Bastard is lucky I didn't bite them off.

All I have in here is a scratchy blanket and flattened pillow. There isn't a bed, so I am forced to sleep on the cold cement floor. In the corner of the room, there's a stainless steel toilet with a sink built into the top of it. I imagine this is what prison is like. How exciting, role play!

Doc never says how long each punishment will be. One day I am down here, and then a few days later he releases me.

Broken fingers... I bet three days, max.

This is meant to teach me a lesson for being such a bad little girl. This bad little girl doesn't learn anything, I treat it more like a boring holiday. Last time they did spice it up for me with some electrotherapy. Although, I think they were trying to 'cure' me. Ha, I am cured! But I went along for the ride, it created some variety in my day. A spicy side trip to this vacation.

A random aide would come get me, leading me to the closed off room on the other side of the basement. Once we get in there, I am given a horrific blue and white medical gown to put on, which I change into, and then I get up on the table where they would strap me down. The first time I panicked, I hate being restrained like this, unless it's by Jasper. I ended up fighting it, and additional aides got called in to hold me down until all straps were around my ankles and wrists.

Then, they put a mouth guard in my mouth, so I didn't bite my tongue or break my teeth.

After that, they connected some monitors to my chest under my thin gown, which connected to machines that would make horribly annoying beeping sounds.

"Iris, this will hurt a little. But it should help you." Doc's voice fills the room, always with that warning.

I can hear his shoes against the cement floor as he makes his way over to me. He is standing by my head now. "Nurse, the electric pads please."

Not another word is said after that. Not even a warning that it's about to begin. The pads were placed on my head and within seconds electricity began flowing through my brain, down into my body. My eyes react by squeezing shut, my body tensed and my jaw clenched. The jolts of electricity only last a few seconds each time. But each time I feel fucking alive. I love this!

The procedure doesn't last long in total before I feel the pads being removed from my head, then chest. My eyes open and I spit out the mouth guard.

Doc walks around so he is within my view, and begins visually examining me as I smile. My eyes light up when I begin cackling. What a fucking rush.

His face quickly turns into a mix of worry and anger. I assume it didn't work as planned, but I hope he tries again... many times!

As I lay on the floor, with the pillow under my head and my sneaker-clad feet up against the wall, I relived the first time I got electrotherapy. I wonder if they have something else fun planned for me since the last few rounds didn't work.

Suddenly, my thoughts and memories are interrupted by a loud scream. What the fuck, who else is down here? I didn't notice anyone else missing before coming down.

Another loud masculine scream fills the space. What are they doing to him?

Now I'm curious. I want whatever they're having.

Getting up from the floor, I walk over to the door and try and peer out of the bars.

"Hello?" I shout, and wait for a response.

It's gone completely silent now.

"Hello?" shouting again.

Still nothing.

So I turn around and make my way back to my floor, laying down when I hear a response. The response sends chills up my spine and tears to my eyes, "Mama, Mama, Mama!"

NO! NO!

"DEX!"

Another scream fills the silence, followed by, "Mama, Mama!"

They have Dex. NO!

Doc's voice follows, "Iris. You are doing this to him. It didn't have to be this way."

Feeling completely helpless, I tumble to the ground and scream.

What was once a peaceful dream, is no more.

It's morphed into a recurring nightmare.

This is now my reality.

He's gone.

They took him from me.

To separate a mother and her child.

It's like sentencing me to be burnt alive.

I hope this is all an illusion.

That my mind has finally betrayed me.

Well, unless you are talking about my mother and
father, they can stay dead.

That remains real.

The rest of it, I need to end. This nightmare, this
horror film, must stop playing in my head.

The scar of this seared into my core.

Dex has been gone since yesterday. I think? I'm not sure, it could be longer.

Time is ticking by while I remain frozen.

I feel weak.

Standing up and functioning is impossible.

My eyelids are too heavy to open. My breathing is shallow.

Twice a day, a person comes in and pushes a pill between my lips.

A paper cup follows, as the water helps it go down my throat.

So maybe it's been longer than a day since they took Dex.

I'm not sure what these pills even are. But I take them.

If he is suffering, then so am I.

Every so often I will hear Jasper.

My sweet, Jasper. The other half of my soul.

He is the calm to my monster.

I'm sure he is trying to talk to me, tell me about his day.

Encouraging me to be strong, but I can't.

But his voice always seems so far away.

Like it's just an echo. So maybe that's not real either.

Just another trick my mind is playing on me now.

Darkness invades. Defeat settling in.
They got me. I put my hands up and surrender.
I'm sorry Jasper.
Please don't hate me.

11

JASPER

It's been four days since they took Dex. Four fucking days.

I don't even want to think about what they are doing to him down in that basement. He has never been down there before. Ris and I have, but never him.

Doc knew exactly how to hurt us. But this, right now, it's only temporary. He caused a shift in power, but we will take it back and get Dex out of there.

After they took him, we stayed as we were for hours on the floor. With Ris snuggled against me. Absolutely heart broken.

Ris had fought so hard to get to him, her knuckles were bleeding from banging so hard on the door. She broke a few fingernails and her eyes were red and swollen from crying. I have never seen her cry before.

As much as this has broken her, it broke me to see her this way.

I couldn't think of what to do next. I just needed her to be ok.

I brought us to the bathroom and placed her delicate body on the floor. I turned the taps on to warm our shower and began removing her clothes, then my own. Picking her back up, I brought us both under the warm spray of the water. Placing her on the shower floor, I grabbed the shampoo and started to wash her hair, then her body, wanting to rid us both of the memory of today. To wash it away. Wash the day off and start fresh in the morning with a game plan.

After our shower, I got her dressed in one of my t-shirts and brushed her hair out. She had stopped crying, but now Savage was silent. No expression on her face. Completely numb.

I dressed us and then brought us to bed. She snuggled right against me, and it made me feel good that I could comfort her like this. I haven't had to in years, not since mother and father.

The next morning, I woke up before Ris and saw our door was open again. I immediately jumped out of bed and ran to Dex's room. It was trashed and empty. Fuck!

Then I went to see Mr. H.

He said after hearing the slam of our door, he peeked out of his room. Eventually he saw the aides drag Dex down the hall, his head slouched over and the toes of his sneakers dragging along the floor. With Karen following behind.

When I asked if Susan was there, he said he didn't see her. Count yourself lucky this time, Susan.

I fucking know Doc ordered this. After the session that day, I knew we'd pushed it. But we had to. We had to show him we wouldn't bend to his demands. Since I'd orchestrated everything in his office, I definitely thought it would be me. Maybe Ris. I never in a million years expected them to take Dex.

Shots have been fucking fired.

Ris hasn't left our room in the four days since they took Dex. She refuses to eat and won't see anyone other than me. She is even letting the aides medicate her. As much as I hate it, I understand. My Savage is a ghost of herself. I need her to come back to me. There is no me without her.

I heard them whispering talk of a feeding tube if she hasn't eaten by tomorrow. I gotta get food into her. If they put a feeding tube down her throat, that's it. They will have complete fucking control of her body and mind. I refuse to let that fucking happen.

She is mine.

I'm walking back from dinner now, alone again.

Some have asked about Savage. I reassured them she is just feeling unwell and will be back to her normal crazy self soon. I don't want them to get uneasy. Their Queen is down in a bad way, but they can never know the extent of it.

Ms.O, I think she senses it, though. She has a killer instinct, literally and figuratively speaking. She gave me her dinner roll to bring back to Ris. The way she looked at me, it was like she was trying to reassure me it would be ok. That she knows and is here for us.

Ris adores Ms. O.

I rake my fingers through my hair as I walk down the hallway to our room. I shout as I go past Mr. H's room, "Did she come out at all while I was gone?"

"Nope. And it's my birthday. She never misses it. Something isn't right. You need to fix her before they do."

Fuck, don't I know it.

"I am working on it, Mr. H." I sound like a fucking pussy, like I'm defeated. I'm not. But I am tired. Only Mr. H knows everything that happened, and since he doesn't leave his room, I can trust him not to spread shit around. As psychotic as the guy is, he means well. I appreciate that.

Walking into our room, she is right where I left her, in bed.

She gets out only to use the bathroom lately.

I have to do something. I need her back. I need Dex back. A member of our family is missing. Another is lost. They are winning. How the fuck am I supposed to fix this? When will this fucking end? I'll never submit to these bastards. Fuck, fuck, fuck!

Sitting on the bed next to her, I pull the dinner roll out of my sweater pocket.

"Savage, Ms. O gave me her roll for you to have. Will you have it? Please, will you try eating for me, Ris?" I plead.

She doesn't move. Doesn't say a word.

"Please. I need you to get strong for me. Dex needs you to be strong for him. We both need you to eat. Please, will you eat?"

Hanging my head, how the fuck am I supposed to get her to eat?

"Ris. I need you to listen to me. They plan on putting a feeding tube in you tomorrow if you don't eat. If they do that, they will control you completely. Who knows what else they will try to pump into you using it. We cannot lose you. Dex, me and the rest of Sutton need you. You are our Queen. Our fucking goddess. I need you back. Please, will you eat this for me?"

It isn't beneath me to beg. I will get on my knees and plead with her if it means she comes back to us. I need her to come back.

Savage, please come back.

12

IRIS

My boy is gone.

They fucking took him.

I failed him. I couldn't stop them.

I'm a terrible mother.

Now he's all alone in that fucking basement because of me. I can hear his scream every time I close my eyes. If only I could have gotten out of this fucking room. I could have saved him. It's all my fault. All my fucking fault.

Dex has to be so scared. My baby.

Am I my mother? Does he hate me? Does he want to kill me like I killed mine when she failed me?

Since they took him, they have been medicating me.

And I let them. Anything to not feel like this anymore.

Dex is in that basement alone.

The basement is cold. It's not only the lower temperature from the brick walls, it's how the energy down there feels. It's where hope dies. Where souls scream.

You lose a part of yourself every time you are sent down there.

Solitary is one section. Jasper and I have been there a time or two on separate occasions. There are no windows and the lights are only turned on if someone's coming down, then they are immediately turned off again. There's no sense of time. You end up sleeping most of the time without having any light to keep you awake. It's not even a good sleep, we aren't given a bed, just a pillow and a scratchy blanket. Your meals are brought at random so you can't even identify time with a meal.. Just more ways of how they try to break you down here.

There's another room just before the solitary rooms. Usually the door is closed. But once it wasn't. It looks identical to solitary, with the addition of a metal table with restraints in the middle of the room. Dex can't be in there. Please don't let him be in there.

Fuck. I can feel it in my bones, though. He's in there. They are hurting my baby. I need to see him. He needs me. I'm supposed to be protecting him.

But I've been here for the last four days instead.

I need to get to him, but for the first time in my life, I feel defeated.I don't know how to get down there.

There's a steel door keeping us apart. It has a deadbolt and one additional steel lock.

I want to scream. But I can't. My body is exhausted. I am exhausted.

Jasper rarely leaves my side. He does only to make his rounds around this place. Keep up appearances and to reassure everyone, or so he says. He always tells me about it when he comes back. People are asking how I am. He tells them I'm just sick and will be back in no time.

He's never gone for long though, and right now, Jasper is here with me.

I'm laying in bed and he is sitting next to me, talking. I can hear him, but I'm not absorbing anything he's saying. He has been so strong for me.

I know he is feeling this, too. The loss in our family. We've been split up. But he is handling it so much better than me.

"Please, Ris. Will you eat?"

He asks me every day . He even brings me food, but I can't.

"Ris. I need you to listen to me. They plan on

putting a feeding tube in you tomorrow if you don't eat. If they do that, they will control you completely. Who knows what else they will try to pump into you using it. We cannot lose you. Dex, me and the rest of Sutton need you. You are our Queen. Our fucking goddess. I need you back. Please, will you eat this for me?"

He sounds so sad. My sweet man.

I lay there. Still not moving. Not reacting. I'm still trying to process everything.

Wait. Feeding tube? I don't need a feeding tube. I'm fine. I'm just not hungry.

"Please. I'll do anything. Just take this roll and eat it. I need you to eat it for me. I fucking love you, Savage. I know you're sad. I know you're hurting. So am I. Our family is under attack and I need you. I need your help fighting this. I need your help figuring out how to get Dex back. We will get him back, Ris. I fucking swear it."

This is killing me. I need to get up.

Because Jasper is right. Sitting here doing nothing isn't helping anyone. Come on Iris. Get up. Move your body. You can do it. The meds make me slower, I've noticed. Even getting up to use the bathroom takes everything in me. Brain, I need you to focus for once. Move my hand.

Come on. Fucking move it!

My hand lifts slowly and I extend my fingers.I feel so weak, but I am able to lightly grip the dinner roll Jasper is holding and bring it to my mouth. I take a tiny bite and then another. It's dry, but I refuse to let them control me. I won't be put on a feeding tube. They won't take my mind. They won't have my body. It belongs to Jasper. He owns me.

"You are doing so good, Savage. Come on. Keep eating. We need you."

Nodding my head, I continue to eat the roll until it's done. Then, turning my head, I need to see his gorgeous eyes. I need his strength. Jasper is the most beautiful man. I bite my lip and smile as mischief fills my head. He knows what this means and smiles back with all his teeth showing.

I'm fucking back and Doc, I'm coming for you first.

13

IRIS

I wake to the sun shining, and there's one thing on my mind.

Get my Dexy back.

I'm still feeling weak from the lack of food these past few days, but I'm not letting that stop me. Nothing can stop me today. Jasper helped me shower this morning, and I got myself dressed and applied my makeup before going to breakfast. I decided to wear all black. This is war and I certainly want to look the part. Black skinny jeans, with a matching crop top and high top converse. Jasper had a baggy white tee on, and I just had to look at him and he knew to change. Silly boy. Doesn't he know black hides the blood? I swear he will never learn.

When we walked into breakfast, I didn't know

what to expect. I let my people down when I disappeared. A queen never leaves her people, but I did.

Jasper told me not to let it get to me, that he had explained to them I wasn't feeling well. He said most people just wanted me to get better.

But it's no secret Dex has been missing too and still is.

I wanted to believe him, but it was hard. I love that they all played along for my sake. I didn't want to be known as the Queen of Sutton that leaves her people when things get hard.

I am not a pussy!

I laugh in the face of dumb cunts and chaos!

I live for this shit. It makes me so fucking horny. I haven't been horny in days. It's devastating just thinking about it.

When I walked into breakfast this morning, one resident yelled, "She's back! Everyone, look, she's back! Our Queen has risen!"

I was shocked. Overwhelmed. They do love me. As much as I love them!

They started cheering and clapping.

I obviously joined in. I am never one to turn down a welcome party.

It was amazing. Even Ms. O was up, saluting the room with her middle fingers high. That woman is a legend. If I am half of what she is at that age, I will consider myself lucky!

Then, the dumb cunt herself walked in. Karen, the master party pooper, ruined it. I didn't initially see her, my back was to the door while I was jumping up and down with excitement. The room got quiet, eyes looked past me and I knew, I just knew it was her. Slowly turning around, my eyes started at her white sneaker-clad feet. This bitch is anything but virginal. Then I moved up her blue scrub clad body, the nurse Karen badge over her tiny chest on the left, then I saw her face. The bitch had the nerve to have a scowl on her face like we were an inconvenience to her. Breaking news Karen, you're an inconvenience to us!

I was as perky as a peach pie when I said, *'well don't you look ravishing today!'*

Karen didn't respond. No welcome back, not even a fuck you! So rude.

She won't kill my mood.

But I am in the mood to kill.

Oh Karen, you haven't seen shit yet. But it is coming.

I promise.

Jasper and I proceeded to eat, then head to the library, where we are now. I am cross-legged on the couch and he is sitting in front of me, his back against it with his legs stretched out before him. Leaning forward, I bring my fingers into his hair and begin scraping his scalp with my nails.

"Fuck Ris, I love when you do that," Jasper moans.

"Normally, I would be all over this. Your dick. Oh, how I have missed him so much, Jasp. But we need to start working on getting Dexy back. It's been too long. They have had him for far too fucking long!"

"Savage, I know you're scared, but we need to be smart about this. If we go all Rambo on the fucking place, the police will be here within seconds. As much as I want to burn this place down, it won't help us in getting Dex back."

Jasper's not wrong. It doesn't mean I like what he's saying, but he isn't wrong. Fuck.

Still rubbing his head, I try to think. I can be subtle, right? I am not always Rambo.

You can do this, Iris. I can totally be incognito, blend in, so no one suspects a thing.

Iris Ashford is a master of blending.

Then I hear Jasper laughing, "No you're not, Savage."

Has our twin connection grown since Dex left? Are we like super twins now? This is incredible.

"Ris, you're saying all this out loud." He is now on his side, laughing even harder.

Scrunching my face, I bring my finger to my chin and think, "Are you sure?"

"Yes. I am so very sure. You are not the definition of incognito, Savage. I hate to break it to you. But thank fuck for that, how boring would that be? Seriously. Zero excitement included in that life. We live for chaos. We are the Queen and King of Sutton. People who blend in could never achieve that. You are the sexiest, most unhinged person I have ever met. That's some of what I love about you. So to say that I am fucking thankful you don't '*blend in*' would be an understatement. You—this—is what gets him hard, Savage. Never change. We will think of something."

Oh, my Satan! This is now the most romantic thing Jasper has ever said to me.

My eyes well with happy tears.This man is going to get the blowjob of his life later!

"Still talking out loud, Savage," Jasper is trying to hide his laugh with one of his hands now.

Not missing a beat, I pounce on him. And that's when it hits me.

I have an idea, it's brilliant! I mean, it is my idea. Of course it's going to be a first class idea.

"Jasp, I think I know how to get Dexy back!" bouncing on him with excitement.

"Lay it on me then."

Kissing his cheek, "We need to see Doc. Now. So get up."

Confusion spreads all over his face. "Savage, we can't just ask for him back. Doc is all about teaching us a lesson. We have to be smart about this."

"We are not asking for him back! Just follow my lead, it's fine. I'm sure it will work. Maybe? No, most definitely, it will. I can see it now. He will bend to our demands and he will fall for our traps. It will be a picture perfect moment when Henry realizes he picked the wrong side and then he will decide to team up with us to take down Karen and Susan." I am salivating at the idea of it. My eyes are wide and my smile feral.

"So. Get. Up. Brother!"

"Fine. Ok, get off me and I'll get up, Savage."

I roll off him and bounce to my feet; he does the same with a little less bounce. I won't dock him points for lack of enthusiasm. He will still get a killer blowjob later.

HA - get it?

Because I'm a killer. Giving a blowjob!

Shaking my head to refocus. Dexy now, blowjobs later.

Grabbing Jasper's hand, I drag him out of the library behind me. We walk down the long hallway to Henry's office.

I'm sad Henry and I will never have our butt sex now. It could have been great. But he blew it, pulling this stunt. Access is now denied!

We reach the door, it's closed. He must be in with a resident trying to cure them, too. Waste of fucking time. How many times do I have to explain this to the man?

Not caring, I burst through the door, into Doc's office and start doing what I do best, causing chaos. " What are you doing to him? Answer me! Our butt sex agreement is off. You blew it, Henry! So, just tell me what are you doing to him, NOW!"

Letting go of Jasper's hand, I have rendered him speechless I think.

It makes me feel proud.

I rush over to Henry, who is sitting in his therapy chair, and jump onto his lap. I bring my lips close to his ear so only he can hear what I say next. "I am no longer fucking around, Henry. I will slit your fucking throat right here, right now. Do you think I have never noticed that letter opener always sitting on your desk?

I will use it. On you. Now tell me where Dexy is and give him back to me."

Slowly pulling my face back, I look at him and wait for his response.

His eyes are wide.

Henry knows I am not fucking around now.

"Get. Off. Of. Me!" Henry is seething.

Looks like I have poked the bear. This is perfect, it's working.

I start laughing hysterically. It's fucking working.

And in this moment I'm also picturing how badly I want to carve up Karen, then use Susan's bones for toothpicks.

If this plan works, and I get my Dexy back. Then the rest will fall into place with those cunts too.

One by one, they will all pay.

14

DEX

Electricity spreads throughout my body. I'm naked, with leather straps around my ankles and wrists. All that is between me and this metal bed is a thin white sheet.

They want me to talk.

They want me to be a puppet for them.

I won't.

I will never betray my family!

Mama is coming.

And when she arrives, she will slit the throats of anyone in her way.

15

JASPER

Two aides are escorting us back to our rooms.

I don't fully understand what Ris's plan was, but I am guessing it didn't work.

I haven't had a chance to ask her yet. I don't trust these fuckers enough to say anything in front of them. We have no idea whose side they are really on. Plus, Doc says he is always watching. That he can always see us. I'm getting more determined to figure out where his fucking spy cams are. Obviously, I know we are in a heavily secured place. Of course, there are cameras… but where does he have them?

Fuck, we will deal with that later.

We are making our way up the grand staircase and to the hallway where our room is. Mr. H pokes his head out, just barely. "She is back from the dead!"

Crazy motherfucker.

"Mr. H. Don't think I have forgotten about your birthday. I swear you will get your present!" Savage tells him, while enthusiastically jumping in place and clapping her hands.

Hearing this brings a smile to the old man's face. What a guy.

It's the little things we do for others that count.

"Keep moving, Ashford," one fucker snaps at Ris.

Closing my eyes, I know exactly what will come next. These guys have no idea how literally she can take things.

"As you wish, commander," Savage takes off skipping down the hall while singing *'just keep moving, moving, moving.'*

"ASHFORD! Get back here, now!" One of the aides yells.

"You assfucks should know better than to tell a fucking crazy person to keep moving. Do they only hire morons here? Is that a prerequisite? You should tell her to cut it out next. Savage is a fucking goddess with a knife!" I shout back at them as they take off after Ris down the hall.

Mr. H takes the opportunity to offer his perspective. "What a magnificent lady."

"That she is Mr. H, that she is. And she is all mine."

Leaving Mr. H to watch what is left of the performance, I walk to our room and wait for her. The two aides are trying to grab her, but Ris keeps ducking under them or hopping around them, still singing, *just keep moving, moving, moving.*

I love her level of crazy. "Savage, why don't you just keep on moving all over my dick?"

Ris stops in her tracks, eyes go wide, and she looks at me. "Say no more, brother. I would love that."

The aides take this opportunity to grab one arm each.

I. See. Red!

This immediately triggers me. The memory of when Father had her tied to the table flashes before me. No one touches her! No one!

Mine! Only me!

"Take your fucking hands off of her. Now! If she tries to end you both, I will not stop her. I would only help her." I say, walking towards them.

They look terrified and immediately freeze.

Ris, full of pride while watching me make my way to the end of the hall, loudly whispers, "Silly boys. Haven't you heard why we are in here? We killed our parents and we will kill you too! I have always wanted a do-over."

What she would give for a do-over. I'll give it to her one day.

At the end of the hall, both step away from her with both hands raised, and Ris closes our distance and wraps her arms around my neck, smiling, "Jasp, my plan didn't work. Let's go play. It will help me feel better."

Leaning in to kiss her, Savage's soft lips connect to mine and immediately I feel the electricity of our connection flow through me. Fuck, I missed her. These past four days have been hell, but I understand it, I do. But still, I have missed her, like this. Pulling back slightly, I whisper against her lips, "I know. We will talk when there are less ears around. We will get Dex back, I swear it."

Ris nods. Her eyes look sad for a moment, but she knows we will get him back.

"Now, mister, you promised me a dick to move on."

Throwing my head back with laughter, "That I did, now get your sweet pussy and tight ass in that room."

"Sir, yes, sir," Ris responds, unlocking her arms from my neck and saluting me. Then she starts making her way to our room. I look back to the aides who are still standing here. "Go! Now!"

Without hesitating, they scramble and take off back down the hall. Motherfuckers, better keep running.

"Jasp, are you coming? My pussy is thirsty for your cock."

This gives me an idea, it's not her pussy that will get my cock this time. We missed Mr. H's birthday, and we owe him a show. This isn't something we normally do during the day. Savage needs this, though. I need this.

"Ris, in the hallway, naked now." I demand.

Staying in place, she starts removing all her clothes and leaves them in a pile at her feet. Savage kicks off her shoes into the room behind her, and makes her way to Mr. H's room. She places her hands against the textured wallpaper opposite his door frame and looks coyly back at me. This girl is delicious. Her milky white skin, '*yours*' in black ink across her neck, that perky fucking ass, and those tits. Desperately pressing against the fabric of my pants, my cock is begging to get out. I undo the button of my pants and my zipper follows as I take the last steps to meet her. "Mr. H, Happy fucking birthday." I shout.

I see from the corner of my eye his head poke out,

"Ah yes, Jasper. Good man, that it is. Thank you both for my wonderful gift. You spoil me each time."

Not responding, my focus is completely on Ris now. Pulling my pants down, then my boxers so they are bunched up at my feet. My cock springs free with precum already dripping from it.

I'm sure Mr. H already has his pants around his knees with his cock in his hand, ready to take this all in. But that doesn't matter to me. What is about to fucking happen here is my priority.

"Savage, bend over and spread your legs."

Standing directly behind her now, I see her pink pussy dripping. Her ass is screaming my name, begging for me to take it. Bringing my hand up to it, I slap it hard. My palm stings as it connects, and the crack of her skin against mine is loud. Ris moans and throws her head back; she lives for this. Her reaction only makes my dick even harder.

"Hmm, Jasp. Again, please," Ris begs.

I love when she begs.

Brushing my fingers along her folds, I then begin to circle her clit several times. She's dripping.

"That's it, my needy slut. I can smell your desperate cunt from here. Your pussy is screaming for me to shove my cock in it. Isn't it? You need your brother to help you, don't you?"

Circling her clit once more causes her to moan again, but instead I stop. It's not time yet. I brush my fingers over her wet pussy once more, then bring my fingers to my mouth. I need to taste her, and she tastes fucking perfect. Like heaven and hell collided.

"You taste so fucking good, Savage," I whisper.

Ris wiggles her hips slightly, the need to fill her ass with my cum, to watch it slowly dripping out of her. It's almost unbearable, "Hmm, more Jasp. I need you." She turns her head slightly and bats her eyelashes at me, with a pouty lip. This fucking girl.

Slapping her ass once more, you see my hand print left behind in red this time, I love seeing my mark on her. Then, grabbing her neck, I whisper in her ear, "I fucking own you."

Without moving, she murmurs back, "And I own you."

I can't wait anymore. Spitting a couple times into my free hand, I use it to lube up my cock. Then, lining it up to her perfect, tight hole, I slowly slide myself into her ass.

"Yes. You. Do." Is all I say before I begin to thrust myself in and out of her. Squeezing her throat tighter, "That's it. You're taking my cock so well. Such a good slut for your brother, aren't you?"

"Fucking always, Jasp. Always," she moans

softly. She's starting to feel the effect of me cutting off some of her oxygen supply. I continue pounding into her. Her tight hole taking me so well, gripping my cock so hard I think with each movement I could explode. Behind me, I hear a few grunts coming from Mr. H. He is the last one I want to hear grunting in my ear. Refocusing on Ris, "That's it Mr. H." She encourages him.

It drives me crazy when she does that while I'm inside of her. But I get why she does it. Such a giver my girl is.

"Focus on me. Only me! It's my cock fucking you right now, not his." I growl .

"Don't worry Jasp, it's only your cock I ever want. Fucking me so hard."

I squeeze her throat once more. "That's right. Me. Only My Cock. Your. Fucking. Cock!"

Savage is gasping for air now. I feel her body begin to tremble as I continue to work her up. I work myself even faster and harder now, giving her the orgasm she is so desperately chasing.

Another violent tremble moves through her. She's gasping now and I know this is it. Letting go of her throat ,I reposition my hands: one at her hip to gain even more control and the other pinching her perky pink nipple. Her orgasm is racing through her body, as she frantically begins to fill her lungs with air again. The sensation rushing through her body is euphoric, so I've heard. Her nerves are tingling and her senses in a frenzy, it makes for an even more heightened level of release.

My own orgasm follows. The tingling moves through my lower spine, my eyes are hooded as I cum inside of her. Never stopping my movement inside of her as ropes of my release coat her.

"Fucking take it. Take it all." I demand, still pounding my cock into her hole.

Ris turns her head to face me, her cheeks are flushed, "I want to feel your cum dripping out of me. I've been such a good, slut. Reward me, Jasp."

Oh, I fucking am.

As it begins to fade, my movements slow and sweat drips down my face. I lean forward, my cock still inside of her and begin kissing down her spine, starting between her shoulder blades and moving my way to her mid back. Goosebumps appear as she trembles under my touch. "I love you, Jasper."

I close my eyes and bring my forehead to her back, "I fucking love you too, Savage."

We stay like this for a moment before I stand up and pull myself out of her. Looking down, I see my cum dripping out of her, along with a tiny puddle of her own on the floor beneath us. I take my fingers and gather some of my release, then bring them to her mouth, where she wraps her lips around them. Sucking off every last drop, using her tongue to get between my fingers. I could explode again just from this. "Fuck, Ris."

She giggles at me while moving her mouth up my fingers and finally releasing them from her mouth, which makes a '*pop*' noise.

"Dessert for dinner." Savage says with a smirk.

Then, turning around to face me, I grab hold of her, our bodies pressed against each other. The smell of sex riddles the air, like two dogs marking their territory. We fucking own this place.

I have all but forgotten about Mr.H behind us, but Ris hasn't. She goes up on her tiptoes and pokes her head over my shoulder and excitedly squeals, "Happy Birthday Mr. H!" causing me to laugh.

"I fucking love you, Savage." I say into her neck as I continue to laugh.

Lowering herself back down, Ris giggles, "Love you too. Now, let's go plan how we are getting our Dexy back!"

"You got it, Savage. But I have to know. What was your plan in Doc's office earlier?"

"I was trying to get one of us taken down to the

basement. Then we could have checked on him, and he would have known he isn't alone. That we are trying." Ris sniffles. Fuck this girl, she meant well. But there's no way they would have taken either of us down there with him.

Holding her tighter, I mumble into her hair, "Don't worry, we will get him back. And I think I have an idea."

16

IRIS

Today is the day!

I'm getting my baby back. It's been DAYS since I saw Dexy. Since these fuckers stole him from me, his family!

My plan didn't go according to plan. Apparently, Jasper was right. I do get a bit 'Rambo', but it was in the name of our family... Plus, it was fun. Really fucking fun. Anyway, it didn't work, Henry saw right through me, bastard. So, we are onto Plan B.

After we gave Mr. H his gift, we moved back inside our room and showered... where we fucked again, but this time his cock was craving my pussy. Jasper fucked me so hard that I ended up biting him in order to muffle my screams. The moment my teeth broke his skin, and the taste of our blood entered my mouth, it turned into a frenzy. For both of us. Our love and desire for pain, for blood and each other, it took over. We devoured one another for hours after that.

After finishing, we both crashed hard. That night, I was exhausted and so were all my holes. They needed to rest and recover for the big day.

Later the next day, we came up with our plan. Well, it's really Jasper's idea, and it's brilliant. Fucking genius!

It has taken us a couple of days to coordinate everything, but we think we got it. So that makes today *the* day!

At this morning's breakfast, we went down as we normally have been since I came out of my state. I did the morning announcements. Tonight is the Grey's finale party in the TV room, which also happens to be our diversion. This should keep everyone busy for an hour or so, giving us time to execute our plan. We are back in our room now changing, "Ris, I think I found where the camera is in this hallway. Last night, after you went to sleep, I cracked that protective cover over the mirror. I chipped off a piece of the mirror, and used that to try and cause a reflection off the lens and it actually fucking worked. It took fucking ages, but I think I got it. It's in the picture at the end of the hall. The eye is the fucking camera. It's how Doc '*sees everything.*' Fucking pervert, probably loved watching us, too."

"The one next to the window? Of the creepy old man? How fitting. So it looks directly down the hall. We just need to make sure we don't look suspicious when we head down tonight. Or Plan B turns into Plan C and I can't, I won't allow that, Jasp. Today is get Dexy back day!" I declare and stomp my foot on the ground.

Jasper walks up behind me, shirtless, and wrapping his arms around my waist. "This will work. They won't suspect shit unless they notice we have disappeared from the party too soon. But I can't see that happening considering last year's finale party. The aides and nurses will want to make sure it runs smoothly. A fucking riot will happen if anything happens two years in a row."

"Where is the piece of mirror you broke?"

"Hidden with my tattoo supplies. Why?" We are standing in front of my mirror; his face is a mix of puzzled and intrigued.

"Get it, I have an idea."

Jasper lets go of me and walks over to where his supplies are hidden under the floorboard. His dark hair falls over his eyes, and he uses his hand to brush it back. The guy looks hot as fuck doing anything. I swear.

"Savage, I know your eye fucking me. Sex after Dex. Got it?"

"Ugh, fine, but you should know my panties are soaked and you are missing out. And sex after Dex, that's catchy. Well played, brother."

He shakes his head at me, but I know he's dying inside now. Jasp stands up with the mirror piece in hand, it looks sharp enough for my idea, perfect! I hold my hand out, "Here, give it to me. And sit your tight ass on our bed."

After passing me the piece of mirror, he turns around and walks to our bed and sits down. His legs spread wide, he raises an eyebrow at me. "What is going on in that pretty, crazy head of yours, Savage?"

"Hush, you like when I'm like this."

"That I do. Come on, give it to me then. Do your worst." He smiles, showing all his sharp straight teeth.

Smiling back, I look into his dark beautiful eyes and make my way over, stopping between his legs once I reach him. Then, I raise the broken mirror shard I am holding and rest it just above his heart. I feel the rush beginning, and I'm sure my pupils are dilated as I take deep breaths through my nose.

Slowly bringing the sharp edge to his skin, I begin to slice into it. Hearing the skin crack beneath my fingers, warm bright red blood dripping out and the smell of copper invading me. All I want to do is lean forward and lick it up until it's all gone, but I can't. Not until we are done.

Continuing my slow, precise movements, I adjust my position just slightly to finish making the cut. Pulling the mirror back from his skin, I admire my work. It is perfect. Then I lean forward and reward myself, licking his dripping blood from where it slides down his abs all the way up to his chest. Jasp doesn't move. His breathing has picked up and I feel him watching me clean him.

Finally, he breaks the silence and my trance, "Why an X?" he rasps.

Standing up tall, I drop the mirror on the bed and grab his face with both my hands. " X marks the spot. And only I have the map that leads to it. It is fucking mine."

"I love your twisted version of romance, Savage. Never fucking change."

Jasper leans in and I think he is going to kiss me. I mean, I kind of deserve it. But instead, he says against my lips, "Sit down, it's my turn."

I am a spoiled girl, giddy with excitement. I

switch spots with him and remove my shirt. I'm not wearing a bra underneath. Jasper makes the same precise movements over my left breast. The sting is satisfying, the cool blood running along my skin, and it's just as exhilarating being on this side of it. His hand is steady as he bites his lip while focusing. No Ris, stop. Sex after Dex.

"Exactly, Sex after Dex. Let me enjoy this, Savage." he laughs at me.

Shit, am I talking out loud again?

"No, but it's written all over your face. Now don't move, I'm almost done."

I listen and stay still while he finishes the second line. Jasp drops the mirror next to me and begins to lap my blood with his tongue, pulling my nipple between his teeth. I grab his hair and keep his mouth there. It feels so fucking good. I don't let him go until he bites me harder than expected.

"Jasper, what the fuck was that?" That was just rude.

"Sex after Dex, then I'll make you scream like the good little slut you are." This bastard, such a tease.

Looking down, I admire his work. We both have matching X's, and only we hold the maps to get there for each other. This is exactly what we needed before entering into battle.

I see Jasper look at the clock. "Ris, we need to get going. It's almost time, so get dressed. We can't be late to our own party."

Jumping off the bed, I rush to the bathroom and take another look at my new art as I turn on the tap. "Jasp, you need to clean yours too before we go!"

"Yeah, I will hurry up." So impatient, men.

I finish washing mine and head out to my closet, throwing on a bra and black tank top to go with my black leggings and black sneakers. Remember folks, you can't see blood on black.

All ready to go, I notice Jasper has put the mirror piece away, and the floorboard is back in place. About time, he makes his way out of the bathroom wearing a black t-shirt, torn skinny jeans and matching black sneakers. He remembered!

"Ready to cause some chaos, Savage?"

"Fuck yes!"

We are in the TV room with the rest of the Grey's fans! How exciting, it's finale night… in more than one way.

Residents have filled the couches and chairs. The aides set up a table full of snacks for us and the TV is on, ready for the top of the hour to hit and the finale to begin. Even Ms. O came. I knew she was a closet fan.

I head to the front of the room. I would have made a speech anyway, but we need to make sure everyone sees us here. Alibi.

"It's finally here, finale night! For once, I would like to thank the staff for not fucking anything up here tonight. For providing us some delightful snacks and for NOT. FUCKING. UP. tonight. We have been waiting all year for this. Now it's time!"

The residents clap with excitement as I take a bow and head to the back of the room to stand with Jasp.

Grey's fills the screen right on time.

We stand in place for ten minutes before sneaking out of the room. Making our way past the nurses' station, like we are using the bathroom down here.

As we turn down the hall to add to our alibi, a hand grabs my arm and roughly pulls me into the restricted staff room we just passed. Jasper, who is beside me, notices right away and follows after me. It's Susan. That bitch.

"Get your disgusting hands off me, Susan!" I screech while shaking my arm in an effort to get her to stop touching me.

Susan closes the door quickly behind us and looks

nervous as fuck. What does she want? What the fuck is happening right now? Does she know? Shit, she is wasting what little time we have.

Finally, the bitch speaks as she releases me. "I know you two are up to something. I don't agree with what they are doing to him… Dex, down there. Here, take this." She digs into her pocket and pulls out two keys.

Jasper examines what she's holding. "What the fuck are these?"

Susan is frantic. Her hands are shaking as she thrusts the keys towards us. "Keys for the basement locks. Take them. Hurry!"

"And why the fuck should we trust you, huh?" I am really fucking suspicious right now.

"You shouldn't. I'm risking everything by giving these to you. I will be fired for giving not just any two patients these, but you two specifically. My career is gone. Dead in the water. License revoked. So just take them, save him! He did nothing to deserve what they are doing to him down there. You two deserve it, but not him." A tear slides down her cheek. Oh, the poor cunt is sad, what a shame.

We still don't trust the bitch, but we aren't going to refuse help at this point. It saves us holding an aide hostage like we planned, threatening their life to get us down to that basement while everyone else is in the TV room, distracted.

"You don't deserve a thank you, or mercy for your role in this. But we will be taking these." Jasper says while snatching them from her fingers and sliding them into his pant pocket.

"There aren't cameras in here, or in any staff only area with the exception of the dispensary for meds. The basement doesn't have cameras either." Susan continues to whimper like the little bitch she is.

Because if there were cameras in the basement, Doc would run the risk of people finding out about the spicy vacations they send me on. They would be either very upset by it, or insanely jealous. I vote jealous.

Jasper clears his throat to get my attention. Looking at him, I make sure we are both on the same page before jumping into my next idea. He gives me the slightest nod. That's my cue.

Moving quickly behind Susan, I jump on her back, my hands on her shoulders, leveraging me to position my legs under her armpits, wrapping them around her chest.

Susan is slow to react as she just only realizes what's about to happen. Her body begins to shake under me as she cries, "I helped you. What are you doing? I gave you the keys. I gave you the keys!"

"Susan. Shut the fuck up. We have had enough of you and your shit. You think giving us the keys redeems you? It doesn't. We just told you, we will show you no fucking mercy. Savage, do it!" Jasper demands.

"My name is Beth!" Susan shouts.

"Yeah? Good for you," I say before I wrap my hands around her head, gripping it tightly, using every ounce of strength I have, I twist her neck in one swift movement. You hear the crack almost immediately, and her head goes limp in my hand. I broke her neck. Bang, one bitch is dead. One to go!

Her body begins to crumble to the floor as I jump off her.

Well, this didn't go as planned, but it was even more fun than I expected!

Jasper rushes me, his lips connect before I can even process. His lips melt to mine, adrenaline coursing through our veins; and this is only just the beginning. He breaks the kiss slightly and whispers, "Savage, let's go get Dex."

17

JASPER

My dick is so hard right now and I want nothing more than for Savage to sit on my face and suffocate me with her pussy.

Shit. No. I need to focus.

Sex after Dex.

Why the fuck did I make this rule?

I love her spirit. How she used every ounce of power behind her to break Susan's neck. The satisfaction on her face when the neck cracked, the sound filling the room. The only thing that would have made it better would have been Ris bathing in Susan's blood afterward. But this one had to be quick; the next one won't be.

Regardless, it is still one of the hottest things I've seen in a while.

That! Right there, that is one of many reasons she is my beautiful Savage.

"Ris, help me move her body to the closet."

I grab Susan's arms and Ris grabs the legs. We need to hide her so we aren't caught before we are able to get to Dex. The closet door is already open, it appears to have a couple coats in it and room for Susan. Between both of us, she is light to carry as we haul her across the room and throw her into the corner of the closet.

Taking one of the coats, I toss it over Susan's lifeless body. It covers enough of her that at first glance they may not even notice… unless it's their coat.

It buys us a little more time to sort out this revised game plan. Because we cannot get caught. I hate even thinking about it. They wouldn't hesitate separating all three of us… for life. Punish us. Give us a death sentence, but to keep us alive and separated is the ultimate life sentence. But, it won't happen, because we won't get caught.

Having the keys to the basement massively helps. We also knew exactly what she was doing when she pulled them out to give to us. Susan wanted to trade a life for a life. Hers for Dex's. That is not how we work. You fuck with one of us; you fuck with all of us.

The bitch had to go.

Someone will eventually find Susan's body. Granted, there aren't any cameras in here, so they'll have a hard time proving it was us. Although, who knows where Doc has other cameras hiding. We will probably have to frame someone else, maybe one of the certifiable crazy motherfuckers they let out of the lockdown wing for tonight's party. Perfect. It will be unfortunate if it comes to that, but completely worth it if it means we aren't separated.

Ris's voice breaks my thoughts. "Jasp, can we go get Dexy now? Please?"

Closing the closet door, I look at her, her bottom lip is sticking out and my killer is cute as fuck right now, "Yeah, let's go before someone comes in here and sees us,"

Reaching my hand out, she grabs on, gripping mine as I lead us through the room. Opening the door the tiniest amount, I peak through the crack to see if anyone is around and I don't see anyone.

"Ris, we have to move quickly and keep quiet. Got it?"

She uses her other hand to zip her lips while nodding her head. That's my girl.

Inching the door open slowly, until the gap is wide enough for us to slide through. At the same time, hoping this door has been recently oiled and doesn't squeak.

Taking a step out of the room and unable to see if anyone is on the other side of the door, I freeze and wait a moment to see if we are clear to proceed. Seconds pass and all I can hear is the echo of the TV. No one has shouted that they've seen us, we are good to keep going. Pulling Ris along behind me, we rush on our tippy toes further down the hall where the basement door is. The only other rooms are the resident bathrooms and a supply closet. There shouldn't be any more obstacles blocking our way to Dex. My heart is racing, palms sweaty, but I can't think of that now. We won't get caught, we are getting Dex back.

With each step, we get closer to the door. It has two locks hanging from it, which, as long as that bitch didn't play us, the keys in my pocket should fit it perfectly. Not only will Ris bring hellfire to this place if they don't fit, I will bring it with her. No. Mercy. Burn this motherfucker to the ground.

"Ris, keep an eye out," I whisper as I reach into my pocket and grab the silver keys.

She nods and turns her head and watches down the hallway. You can faintly hear the TV is still playing. Time is not on our side, we have to move.

Putting one key in the top metal lock, it goes in

smoothly, quickly I turn it and it pops open. Thank fuck.

Leaving the key inside it, I move to the bottom one. It's older and much bigger, with some rust around the edges. I grab the second key from my pocket, but it's much harder to get in. Shit. I fumble with it, wiggling it while I push it in. "Come on, go in. Fucking go in," I mumble. Ris looks back at me, "It's ok, keep watching for people." I instruct and she listens without a fight. This is the most serious I've seen her since that night when we were fifteen.

I continue to fumble with this old shitty key, it's going in, but slowly and I don't want to force it in case it breaks. "Jasp, hurry up!" Ris mutters. Her patience is growing thin, and frankly so is mine.

The key is so close to being fully in, and I can hear my heart beating in my ears in anticipation. Blowing out a breath, I push in the final piece and delicately start to turn.

"Jasper!" Ris hisses.

"For fuck's sake, I'm going."I hiss back at her. I know she's getting anxious and so am I. We have been standing here for far too long. At any time, someone can walk by and we can kiss Dex and our freedom goodbye.

The click of the lock unlatching fills the hall. I let a sigh out of relief. Thank you, Satan.

I reach to take both locks out of the latches, but Ris beats me to it. She knows we are racing against the clock and is wasting no time. Once both are taken off the door, she passes them to me to hold. We can't leave them lying here, too much of a risk, so we have to bring them down with us.

Having the locks in one hand, I open the door frantically with the other. The realization that we are getting Dex back is kicking in, as so is more adrenaline. If this is how I feel, I can only imagine how Savage is. She already has a kill under her belt tonight.

Ris ducks under my arm and slips past me to run down the stairs. There is a single hanging lightbulb over the stairway leading down to the darkness below. Wasting no time, I close the door behind me and follow after her. Our feet hitting each step echo around us. Savage reaches the bottom first, her head moving side to side before she takes off into the dark space. Shit, where did she go?

Chasing after her in the same direction, but I can't see a thing. "Ris, where the fuck did you go?"

"Jasp, this way! There is light shining under the door."

Squinting my eyes as they adjust to see in the dark, I catch a glimpse of light from the direction I heard her talking.

Fuck, please let it be this easy. Please let him be in there.

I hear the doorknob turning back and forth, "It's fucking locked! Do something Jasper. You have to do something!" Savage shouts at me in a panic.

"Keep your voice down and move out of the way," I bark back at her. She moves quickly to the side as I bring my foot up and kick the wood door in front of me. It doesn't break on the first attempt, so I try again. I hope he's behind this door, but it's still too quiet down here to tell. Giving it another hard kick, with all my power behind it, the door swings open. The light from the room shines through the now broken door frame as Ris runs through it as I follow behind. I don't even realize she has stopped as I run into her. I grab her shoulders so she doesn't fall forward with me landing right on top of her. She gasps, and at first I think it's because I almost took her out, but then once I look up and see what she sees, I realize it's not. Savage has her hands over her mouth, stunned by what she sees before her. "Oh my Satan... Dex!"

18

IRIS

I'm frozen in place. My eyes are wide, heart beating rapidly, completely shocked by the scene before me. What have these fuckers done to my Dexy? I need a fucking knife. Where is a fucking knife? I am going to slit everyone's throats for doing this to him.

My baby, my pet. My Dexy.

He is naked, a sheet between him and the table. There are leather straps around his wrists and ankles. He has welts covering his entire figure that look like they could be from a belt buckle. My eyes move up his body, examining every inch. There is dried blood crusted around the tips of his fingers, and a few nails from each hand seem to have been removed.

On his chest there are red circle burn marks. It

reminds me of the electric pads they used on me when I was in solitary.

And these people have the audacity to think I'm crazy? To think I am a danger to fucking society?

At least we are honest about it!

They are the dangerous ones, liars and frauds!

"Mama, Mama, Mama, Mama…"

Hearing his voice, my eyes immediately look to his face. He is in agony. There are headphones covering his ears, his eyes are shut, squeezed tightly together.

My baby. What have they done to you? These fuckers know why he's here! They know what his sister used to do to him!

My blood is boiling. I feel a wet substance on my cheek, but I don't move to see what it is.

"Mama, Mama, Mama, Mama, Mama!"

Jasper's face enters my line of sight, obstructing my view of Dex. His hands on my shoulder and his voice sounds like it's off in the distance. "Ris, hey, hey, focus on me. Look at me. You got to snap out of it. You have to stop screaming. They will hear us. I need you right now. Dex needs you right now. Savage. Please."

I'm not screaming… Am I?

Bringing my hands to my face, the first thing I

feel is water on my cheeks, running down to my chin. Touching my lips now, I feel my mouth is open. Jasper is right, I must be screaming.

"Savage, please. We need you. Please, focus on me. I've got you. We've got you." Jasper pleads. His voice is becoming clear and present. Closing my mouth, I hear the background noise stop.

"That's it, good girl. Come back to me."

Shaking my head, I blink rapidly a few times in an effort to bring myself back to the present. Back from the shock of seeing someone I love—my family—laid out naked and tortured before me. All because of me.

He is a good boy. He didn't deserve this. I want to scream again, but I internalize it instead. Jasper is right, we can't let them find us. Not before we get Dexy the fuck out of here.

"I'm here. I'm back. Jasp… they didn't need to do this to him. Why? It should have been me. It should've been us! Not him!" I shriek, so many emotions are running through my body. From rage to sadness to anger to mother fucking revenge.

"Ris, I know. We will. I fucking promise. But we got to help Dex now." Jasper reassures me. Shit, I was talking out loud again. But he's right.

Taking a deep breath in, I exhale and it's go time.

"I'm back. I'm here. I got this, we have got this.

Let's get Dex. We have to be careful and gentle. I'm not sure what shit has come back to the surface from what they have done to him…"

Jasper just nods his head in understanding when Dex's voice brings our attention back on him.

"Mama… Mama…" Dex cries out.

Jasper turns around and I rush around him. We need to get him the fuck out of here. Not wanting to startle him, I go to his head first and remove the head-phones from his ears. All you hear is loud heavy metal coming from them. His dark hair is disheveled, and the imprint from the headphones remain in his hair and on his ears. These fuckers have been torturing every sense he has.

They are monsters.

Dexy's body begins to shake vigorously, and his screams for me pick up speed, leaving his mouth.

Touching his shoulder gently with my hand, I lean down and whisper in his ear, "Dexy, baby, I'm here. We are here. It's ok. Dexy… shhh, Mama's here. Jasper is here."

Staying with Dexy, I continue to whisper in his ear while Jasper removed the restraints around his limbs. I tell him that we are here. That I am here. Mama has come to save him. "Jasp, where are his clothes ? Do you see them?" I ask. Jasper rushes over to the cabinets off to the side against the wall, and begins rummaging through them.

Dex's eyes are still shut. He is still murmuring 'Mama' as he reaches his trembling hand to my head. He turns his slightly and I rest mine on his.

"Got 'em, Ris." Jasper shouts., I hear his footsteps make his way over to us.

"Hey Dex. I'm so sorry. This should have been me. You did nothing to deserve this. You did nothing wrong. You are so fucking strong. We love you, Dex. Now buddy, can you open your eyes for us? I know Ris would love to see them." Jasper coaxes.

"Mama…"

"I'm here baby. I am so sorry. Mama will take care of them. Every last one. I fucking swear it, baby boy. But I need you to open your pretty eyes. Can you do that for me, for us?" I encourage Dex.

Dex takes a deep breath in, then slowly opens his brown eyes.

Whispering to him now, "That's it, Dexy. That's my boy,.I'm here. Jasper is here." Then kissing his forehead.

"Buddy, can we get you dressed? I know you have been through hell. And I hate to rush you. I fucking hate it. But we need to hurry, we can't get caught. We have to finish this."

Dexy closes his eyes once more, then nods.

He knows unless it was important and urgent, we would not dismiss him or rush him to snap out of this and move. He knows us. We are not those people to him. But if they find us down here, helping get him out. That's the end of us. Forever.

Before sitting up, he grabs my hand and kisses my palm. "I love you too, Dexy. Mama loves you so fucking much."

He lets go of my hand, and I step back, removing my hands from his shoulders. I turn around to give him some privacy to change. I know I have seen him naked, but not like this. He deserves the privacy to get dressed. Jasper stays next to him, passing him his clothes.

"Savage, you can turn around," Jasp says softly.

Not wanting to startle Dex, I approach him slowly, but he rushes me and picks me up. His arms wrapped around me, and mine around him, "Mama."

Sniffling, "Baby I'm here. Mama is here. And we will get these fuckers, one by fucking one. I promise. We are going to have so much fun!"

We stay like this for a few moments before he puts me down. Walking over to Jasper, they embrace. I love this. My guys, my family, reunited.

Those motherfuckers who tried to separate us,

who tried to destroy us… I am going to slowly drain the blood from each and every single person who touched him. They will not get the pleasure of a quick death like Susan. That bitch deserved more. I used to daydream about how I would do it. Hang her from the rafters by her hair, with rope. Staple her mouth shut so I wouldn't have had to hear her complaining, and begging for me to stop. Cut her eyelids off so it would force her to watch me and everything happening to her. But we had to keep it clean this time. Jasper didn't need to speak it; his face said it all.

He was right. Dex was our priority. And finding him like this, I wish we had gotten here sooner. These mother fucking people are going to pay with skin, blood and screams!

They better run and hide.

One, Two… we are coming for you!

19

JASPER

My Savage shows her emotions clear as day on her face, and by her actions, but mine hide deep inside. Right now, though, my demon is surfacing. He wants out to play. I can hear him telling me to kill, kill, kill! He is tempting me with bloodshed, mischief, and vengeance. Everything I want. Everything I *crave*. He has it laid out on a fucking silver platter, ready for me to grab. And this time... I'm going to listen.

Ris is standing with Dex, holding his arm and snuggling close up to him.

"Dex, I need to know. Who hurt you? Who left these marks all over you? Was it Doc? Karen? Susan? An aide? Jesus himself? I need to know," asking as I make my way to the door. I know he won't respond verbally, so stopping in my tracks, I turn around. Turning my head to look up at Dex, I list their names. Doc, he nods. Karen, he nods. The same aides that escorted Ris and I up to our room, and then dragged his beaten, limp, and unconscious body down the goddamn hall on the day he was taken. Dex nods. No point mentioning Susan; that bitch has been handled already.

Savage reads my mind and begins to explain to Dex how the chaos has already begun. "Dexy, we don't have much time, so we have to get moving. Don't worry, we already took care of Susan. She tried to buy her freedom by giving us the keys to get down here. She tried to bribe us for mercy, but neither can be bought if you hurt one of our own. We set up the Grey's finale party, made an appearance, then snuck out. Then I snapped her neck and killed the bitch while she was screaming, '*My name is BEEETH*' like we give a fuck what your stupid fucking name is. She was so pathetic, Dexy. You know how annoying I find it when they get like that. So she is now Bye Felicia," Ris finishes explaining in true Ris style, while I still am looking up at Dex. I am silently acknowledging and absorbing the information he gave with his single nods. The three of us know it can only lead to one thing.

"Well, brother. Shall we?" Ris speaks up.Her pupils are dilated, a mix of excitement and rage radiating off her. She has had but a taste of something we haven't had in years and needs more.

Blood, Murder and Mayhem.

I am not one to deny her what she truly desires. So, yes sister, we shall.

IRIS

Brother dearest leads the way back through the dark basement towards the narrow stairs. Right now, he is calm and calculated, our leader, but when the time comes… Jasper will be just as involved in the mayhem. He knows how to keep his demon tame until it's time to unleash him.

His is such an obedient demon. Mine, not so much. My demon is fifty shades of fun and carnage. I smile at the thought, my demon and I always have the best time together.

I've latched onto Dex's arm as we follow Jasp. My Dexy is a part of me that has been returned and I am whole again. I fucking missed him. I know that if I don't hold on to him, I will jump past Jasper and rain mayhem down on these pieces of shit before it's time. You may have noticed that my impulse control is severely lacking. It's more fun that way though!

My body is vibrating with adrenaline and antici- pation of what is coming. Holding Dexy is grounding me, for now.

"Once we get to the door at the top of the stairs, I will make sure the coast is clear. Then we go straight to Doc's office. No stopping. Not even if one of those morons tries to stop us. We go. Got it?" Jasp calls back to us.

"Sir, yes, sir! I love when you get all bossy with me." It's only the truth. I would drop to my knees and suck his delicious cock right now if I could. His stern, authoritative, deep voice commanding me. It fucking makes me melt.

"Hmm, we definitely got it, brother."

Hissing back at me, "Fuck Ris, not now. You can be my horny slut after we finish this."

"Fine. You're the boss." I sigh in disappointment.

Jasper takes soft steps up the stairs, one at a time and not rushing it. We follow his lead. Dex nudges me ahead of him so I am sandwiched between them. It's cute when they try to protect me. Once we reach the top, Jasper stops just ahead of me, slowly opening the basement door and peaking through the thin crack to check the hallway. We stay like this for what seems like minutes, it's completely silent, which makes me uncomfortable.

The wait is too long. I mumble, "Can we go?"

Jasper waves his hand back at me, and continues to concentrate, looking through the crack of the door, then nods as he opens the door wider and sneaks through it. We follow, it's time for stealth mode!

As we all quietly make our way down this hall, we faintly hear two very familiar voices speaking. "Where the fuck are they?"

Then another one responds, "Can't we get Doctor Peters to check the cameras?"

"No, he's in a session. You know the rules. Plus, it's not an emergency. They probably just snuck away to fuck. It's no wonder they are here; fucking your sibling is not normal."

This immediately triggers our past, back when we were fifteen years old. After each time we got caught, then belittled and punished for loving each other. Mother and Father would tell us we weren't right in the head, an embarrassment to society and disgusting.

We are not!

We are two parts of the same depraved soul. Never to be separated, even after death.

Why doesn't anyone fucking understand this?

My chest begins heaving. My vision and thoughts tunnel. There is no more reasoning with me. I have fucking had it with these people thinking they are better than us. Thinking that they can torture us, mark us, drug us, fucking judge us and there won't be repercussions? We are in a fucking asylum. We are the crazy and the unhinged. The incurable, dangerous creatures society has locked away. We are the people your parents warn you to stay away from. And these morons want to test us?

Without hesitation, I run past Jasper towards the voices... the ones down the hall, not in my head. Reaching the end of the hall, I see the two aides standing in the main area where the grand staircase is and the house branches off into other wings. Their backs are to me, and they are standing in front of the hallway that leads to Henry's office and only a few feet in front of me

Wasting no time, I quickly tip-toe towards them. Nothing better than a sneak attack. Behind me, I can hear Jasper swearing under his breath. Oops! He will get over it, but only after he punishes me. I hope!

There is a small wooden table against the wall with a lamp on it. Sadly, I have tried to pick it up before, but it is screwed to the table. Fuck, what am I going to use? I mean, I could break their necks, but I want to have fun with them.

Then, nearly missing it, I see a pen hiding behind the lamp. We aren't allowed stationary unless supervised, so this had to have been left here by accident. An accident which is now to my benefit and advantage.

It's also a sign. The universe *wants* me to kill them for their part in what happened to Dex, and for sounding exactly like Mother and Father.

Grabbing it, I remove the cap and pass it to Jasper ,who I know is behind me. As much as he is annoyed with me right now, he also wants in on this.

I get right behind the shorter guy with blond short hair. Which normally wouldn't matter, but the bright red of his blood will paint his hair perfectly. I can't wait!

I have the pen clenched tightly in my hand, and with all my fucking might, I stab it into his neck. His hands go to where I punctured his skin, and a gasp leaves his mouth. But I don't stop there. In quick succession, I repeatedly continue stabbing his neck. Reaching one arm around his head, I pull him back toward me, and he loses his balance, falling back. I jump out of the way, then leap atop of him. My legs are on either side of his torso and I keep stabbing him.

Blood is spraying me with each puncture. I can feel the warm crimson blood splattering on my face and in between my fingers. Not stopping even as I glance up, I see Dex has hold of the other aide. He is a tall, ugly bastard with dark hair. Jasper has stuck the pen cap into one of the guy's eyes, and it remains there sticking out as blood rushes down his ugly face.

I continue to watch Dex and Jasp, mesmerized by their movements, and my target begins choking on his own blood. What a shame, but not really. He lets out a big cough as he tries to gasp for air that he will never get, and blood runs out of his mouth. It flows down his chin and the side of his face. I stop stabbing and just watch, relishing in the chance to witness his life leave his eyes. I never got that opportunity with my mother and father. Tilting my head to the side, I examine his face. He is still holding his throat where the multiple punctures are, but his hands are not actually doing anything to stop the inevitable. His eyes are wide, tears are pouring out of them, and his mouth is still open, like he's trying to catch one last breath while he continues to choke. Faintly, he sneers, "You bitch." Which I respond by rolling my eyes. Really, that's it?

"Oh boo hoo, you hurt my feelings." I say sarcastically. I am kind of disappointed; I thought he would do better than that for his last words. At least Susan screamed.

Focusing back on him, and looking into his eyes now, I can see the exact moment when life begins to fade. The pupils swell and the whites of his eyes begin to look almost gray. Emptying out onto the dark wood floor beneath us. Then he is gone. His chest has stopped moving. His hands go limp and his eyes remain wide, but the glossy wetness that was once there is gone.

What a magical moment. I smile, pleased with myself. I need more. It's been too fucking long.

Looking up at Jasper and Dex, I see as Jasper breaks the other aide's jaw. His hands are inside of his mouth, one gripping the top, the other gripping the bottom as he quickly rips them apart in opposite directions. He screams, and Dex quickly puts his hand over the gaping hole where his jaw once was, to muffle the sound. Jasper lets go and steps back, admiring his work. The bottom part of the jaw is just hanging there, loose and flapping against his neck, tongue and teeth on full display.

This is such beautiful art coming to life before me. Where mine is bold and flowing—pun intended. It has depth, it's dark and dramatic. It doesn't stop there. Dex kicks the back of the aide's knees, causing him to fall.

Jasper likes toying with his victim, walking back towards him slowly. Calculating.

"Ris, your pen?" He says, while still concentrating on his prey. I stand up and walk towards him, pen in hand, and give it to him. It is already covered in blood, which now has rubbed onto Jasp's hand. Jasp nods his head at Dex, signaling him to remove his hand from the aide's mouth. He is no longer screaming. I think he is in shock. Dex removes it. Then, in a twist of events, Jasp shocks me.

Instead of using it as a sharp weapon like I did, Jasper shoves the bloodied pen down the aide's throat and he instantly starts to choke. You can see his chest reacting. Fighting for his life, he is trying to cough up the object out of him. It won't work. Jasper pushed it all the way down, and it's not moving. His death will be slow and painful. I like it. It's perfect. Jasper never got to deliver it slowly to mother. It makes me happy that he can do it this time.

Jasper stands in front of the dying man for a few more moments before breaking his trance and moving towards the other aide. Whispering to me, "We have to move them."

We can't get caught yet.

Jasper throws him over his shoulder and walks back to the hall we just came from, and Dex follows with the other, holding him bridal style. Once they both disappear down the hallway, I am left standing alone here examining the dismay remaining. Thankfully, we wore black. If anyone were to see me right now with a white shirt on, it would only alarm them. We aren't done yet. So always remember, black doesn't show blood.

Dex and Jasp come through the opening and head towards me. I ask, "Where did you put them?"

"Threw them down the basement stairs."

"What about the mess?" I ask innocently, batting my eyelashes, knowing full well I may have gotten just a tiny bit carried away.

"You are in so much fucking trouble. But that's for later. This mess… will have to stay. At least if people see it, they won't question where it came from, even if there are no bodies"

Smiling back at him, this is his way of saying he loves me. I can't wait to be punished later!

I begin humming and skipping down the hallway leading to Henry's office. This is so exciting! Not knowing how much time we have left until people start leaving the TV room, we have to hurry. The window is closing on the element of surprising Henry. I can't wait!

You hear Dex and Jasper chuckle behind me as they follow.

Three, Four... Doc, we are coming through your door.

20

JASPER

I t's blood for blood, Doc.

Dex bleeds, you bleed, mother fucker.

My hunger for revenge is increasing by the second. Having had a taste already, I need more. We need to make them all fucking pay.

Savage reaches his door at the end of the hallway first. Dex and I both pick up our pace, so we are there when she opens it. We overheard the aides saying he was with a patient and wouldn't be watching the cameras. If Doc has a heart attack seeing our faces barge in, I do not want to miss that.

Jumping on the balls of her feet, "I'm so excited!" Ris declares as her hand reaches for the silver doorknob. Turning it swiftly, she throws the door open the moment she hears the latch click.

"Oh, Doctor Peters! You have been a very, very bad boy!" Savage sings into the room as she walks in.

Doc's eyes widen at her presence, then sees me walk in behind her.

"What do you two think you're doing here?" Doc shouts from his chair. Then, right on cue, Dex walks in. I swear you can see his heart drop when it registers what he is seeing before him.

"How? How? Tell me!"

Savage is laughing maniacally, then, instantly, with a blink of an eye, she flips her switch and snaps at Doc's question. "That is none of your business, HENRY! Because you have been a very bad boy. And Bad. Boys. Don't. Get. REWARDED!"

Doc sits there silently, absorbing what is unfolding before him. Then he stutters, "Joseph, I think... I think that's the end of our session." Joseph, who looks incredibly bored anyway, gets up from the couch without a word. I grab his arm before he is able to leave. "Not a fucking word." He smiles back at me, his eyes almost look black, and nods. I think he is in here for pyro tendencies with a side of mutilation, so I'm sure the guy is just hoping he gets a piece of the action later. I don't blame him. This shit is fun. Seeing their faces when they realize what is about to happen is part of my addiction. As the realization washes over them and they know there is no way out, it's fucking beautiful. Watching their emotions surface when the pain is inflicted, you can see who a person really is in their final moments.. And that is what I crave. Where Ris craves all the other aspects.

Joseph is finally gone, closing the door behind him as I walk up next to Ris. "Why don't you sit on his lap, Savage. Can you do that for me?"

She turns to face me, smiling with blood splatter still on her face. "Of course." Then, leaning in, she gives me a quick kiss on the lips. I lick mine after, faintly tasting the copper from the blond aide's blood. I reward her with a slap on her ass, which makes her squeal, then jump slightly from the force of it.

Ris wastes no time positioning herself on Doc's lap while he is still sitting in his chair. Placing a leg on either side of him, she wraps her arms around his neck while he examines her face.

"Do you like it, Henry? It's art." She enthusiastically tells him about the blood decorating her body.

"Whose? Whose is it?" Doc, you are in no position to be making demands. None of us reply. All three sets of eyes focus directly on him. He has to feel it. Even the air in the room has changed, it feels more stale. The inevitable end is approaching.

"TELL ME DAMNIT!"

Ris turns her head slightly from side to side, trying to read him. Doc's eyes are shifting back-and-forth and he speaks up again. "Iris Louise Ashford: Narcissistic Personality Disorder; Homicidal Tendencies; Dependent Personality Disorder and Histrionic Personality Disorder. Sociopath!"

Ris starts clapping gleefully. "Yay! You got them all! One gold star for you, Henry!"

Doc completely ignores her and continues. "Jasper Aston Ashford: Homicidal Tendencies; Dependent Personality Disorder; Antisocial Personality Disorder…"

I'm sick of hearing him spewing this bullshit. I'm not sure exactly what he is trying to achieve by listing off all our diagnoses. Humanize us, or some shit? Well, it isn't going to work because we know what we are. I'm done listening, "ENOUGH!"

The room goes silent, all eyes are focused on me. Doc has a clock on his desk, and I can see there is only fifteen minutes left before the finale is over. Fuck, fuck, fuck, we are quickly running out of time. But I don't show my worry. He would only take advantage of it.

Ris is closely observing me. No words need to be exchanged between us. To anyone else watching, my face is blank, stone cold, and unreadable. But not to

Savage. She can read me when no one else can, she can sense what I'm feeling and right now, I feel the weight of executing this plan on my shoulders. Time is no longer on our side.

And right on cue, Ris shifts her focus back to Doc. He is focused on me, but she grabs his face with her hand, forcing him to look solely at her. "Now, Henry. Don't think I have forgotten about what a bad fucking boy you have been! Dexy told me all the naughty things you have done to him. And you know the rules Henry, you fuck with one of us, you fuck with all of us! HE. IS. OUR. FAMILY! You and your fucking people touched him! Marked him! Left him naked and alone with loud fucking music invading his ears. And strapped to the fucking table!" Ris shrieks at him. I can see the side of her face is red and her chest is heaving.

Ris holds her free hand out. "Someone get me the gold plated letter opener that is on his desk! NOW! It's always laying on his goddamn desk. Taunting me during each useless session, '*Iris, come play with me*', '*Iris, I want to be painted in blood too*'."

Dex is the one who walks to the desk and passes the letter opener to Savage. I notice Doc also has a picture frame next to it, which gives me an idea. Rushing over to where Dex is, I grab the picture frame and smash it onto the ground, smashing it into pieces, including the glass on the front. Taking a piece, I motion for Dex to pick one up as well. He deserves this.

As we both walk around the desk to stand back by Ris, she is already toying with her prey. She's brushing the opener along his exposed skin, across his forehead, past his cheek, under his chin, then pressing it against his throat. She is laser focused.

Before my beautiful Savage can get carried away without us, I step up and thrust the piece of glass I'm holding into his hand resting on the armrest. He instantly screams like a fucking pussy. This is going to be fun. Dex hurries behind Doc and covers his mouth to muffle the noise until he is done. After passing me his piece of glass, Dex uses his other hand to hold Doc down. Dex is a strong motherfucker. Doc isn't going anywhere.

Taking the second piece, I hold it up to his face and begin to carve into Doc's forehead. I've entered a trance-like state, hyper-focused on each cut and each letter. It's like a drug addict getting a fix. The moment it enters their veins, they feel entranced. This is my version of it. It feeds my demon.

"Doc, I think we need a session. Our 'Homicidal

Tendencies' are starting to show, aren't they, brother?" Ris is fucking loving this.

As I continue to carve, blood begins to trickle down his face and Ris gasps when she notices what I'm writing, *'BAD BOY'*.

Immediately, she gets giddy, bouncing up and down on Doc's lap while clapping. "Jasp, it's absolutely perfect! Now everyone will know, Henry. You are a bad fucking boy!" Her declaration makes me chuckle. I finish the Y at the end, then toss the bloodied glass to the ground. Examining my hands, I noticed a cut along my palm from where I was holding it. Without hesitating, I grab Savage's face and kiss her. Devouring her lips, invading her mouth with my tongue while she moans into my mouth. Then, moving my hand from her cheek, down her neck past where our vow is, to her chest, I leave a stream of bright red behind.

Savage pulls back slightly and mumbles against my lips, "My turn." Without another thought, she takes the letter opener and slashes her palm; her eyes widen as the adrenaline courses through her body. Then she places her hand on my face, following the same path on my skin while biting her lip in concentration. Once she removes her hand from my chest, she grabs my wounded palm, and clasps our blood-soaked hands together. "Blood for blood. Mine and yours"

"Oh Dexy! Can you please pass me his stapler?" Ris requests. Dex steps away from holding Doc down and walks towards the desk, taking the stapler and heads back toward us. I reach my free hand out. "Savage, what do you need me to do?"

"You three are deranged! You are animals! You won't get away with this. I'll make sure you end up separated and in a maximum security prison for the rest of your lives!"

Ris hates when they get like this. It makes her blood boil.

"Dex, please hold his arms down. Jasper... Staple his eyelids open." Dex smiles. Like us, he loves this shit, but for the most part, he keeps it contained. Dex holds Doc's wrists down against the armrest of the chair he is still sitting in. Doc tries moving his head back and forth to make it more difficult for me, but Ris is all over him. Holding his face still and digging her nails into his skin, "Stay. Still!"

Using my thumb and forefinger, I grab ahold of his eyelid, using his lashes to pull the thin piece of skin up towards his eyebrow. Flipping the stapler open, I position it where I need it and jab it into his skin. Doc screams, loudly. It surely could burst an eardrum, and has no doubt alerted anyone who is nearby. Fuck.

Moving quicker now, I grab his other eyelid and repeat the motions, then jab the stapler into his skin. Both lids are now stapled open. Doc's eyes look like they could bulge out, but they won't, unless we make them.

Behind me, I hear the door open. Dex looks up first, and the most sinister smile I have ever seen on his face appears. His teeth are showing and chaos invades his eyes.

There is no need to turn around. "Welcome, Karen."

Five Six... are you ready for the pain we inflict?

21

IRIS

"Dexy, my sweet boy. It's ok. You can let it out. She did terrible things. She deserves it. Mama will not judge you."

Henry thinks this is the best time to speak. It's not, but he does it anyway. "Karen. Call the police. Hurry. Go. Run!"

Will this man ever shut up?

Shit, he is annoying. It would have never worked between us.

I swiftly grab his tongue before he is able to close his mouth after telling our newest guest to run. Taking the letter opener still in my hand, I stab it through his tongue. Henry tries to shout, but it's weak. Just like him. The letter opener blocks him from being able to speak properly now. Thank fuck.

Ropes of blood flow down his chin.

I can't believe I was ever going to let him have bum sex with me. Dodged a bullet with that one.

Pulling my head back slightly, I am able to get a full, proper view of his newly decorated face. It's beautiful. It's art.

While I was busy with Henry, I didn't even notice Dex disappearing. At first I hear the door close, then the click of the lock, breaking my focus on Henry. My baby boy is handling his business. I am an extremely proud Mama right now.

"Don't you try anything, Henry. I am going to turn my body around so I can watch my Dexy in action. I've never seen it before. If you try anything, except for also watching, I will stab you dead with a pen. And before you think I'm bluffing, I'm not. Just ask your little blond aide! Oh, wait… you can't. I already did that to him." I tell him while laughing in his face. Then, once I've slapped his cheek a couple times for good measure, I rotate my body to get a better view of the show.

Karen is standing there like a stuttering idiot, "The…The Ashfords… Missing... Dex… How?"

"Dexy, find something in Henry's desk you can use. Don't worry, Jasper will make sure she doesn't move." I instruct. He walks back over to the desk and begins rummaging through the drawers.

Jasper taunts her now, "Karen, I insist, please take a seat on the couch. It's time for your first session."

Karen doesn't move. Her eyes are still wide and she continues her ramblings.

"Yes Karen, we are the Ashfords. All three of us. But today, you can call me doctor. Now tell me, why are you such a cunt?"

Jasper pushes her forward, "I really do insist that YOU. SIT. THE. FUCK. DOWN!" She stumbles forward a couple times, before finally reaching the couch and sitting down.

"Now, I already have your diagnosis. No need to waste anymore time telling me how you feel, because I don't care. I believe you are suffering from Dumb Cunt Disease. You may have heard of it. Some people call it DCD. In case you were wondering, yes, it is pronounced as 'dicked'. Unfortunately for you, there is no cure. No one wants to dick a dumb cunt. You must be put down in order for it not to spread."

You can see the exact moment when the reality of the current situation sets in. Her mouth drops and she shrieks. "What have you done to him? HENRY! You have to stop this! You can't allow them to take over like this!"

Laughing at her frantic stupidity, "Henry is unable to speak right now. He is only here to observe. We

talked before you arrived, and he agreed with me."
Karen is still in disbelief and tries to get up to leave,
but Jasper stops her and pushes her back down. Dex
then steps forward with his supplies; amongst them
are a pair of scissors, a staple remover, a notepad and
a bottle of pills. Dex has keys in his other hand, along
with a cool flip-trick lighter which he tosses at Jasper
to hold on to, then he dumps the rest on the ground in
front of Karen.

"Dex, what kind of pills are they?" Jasper inquires
after pocketing the keys and lighter. Dex reaches
down and holds the bottle up to him, and Jasper reads
it aloud. "Vicodin. Fuck, yes."

Dex drops the pills down and gets right to work.

Karen screams in hysterics, "You can't do this.
Don't you know who I am? They will lock you up.
They will execute you."

All I hear is '*blah, blah, blah*'. Jasper has a plan.
Nothing is happening to us.

Dex stands over her. He is much taller than her
and much bigger. Karen is like a tiny cockroach
trying to scurry away on the couch. Dex takes the
staple remover in his hand and rapidly pushes it
against her cheek, squeezing it shut. The sharp
prongs on it puncture her skin, and her immediate
response is to move away, pulling her head back.

Proving my diagnosis correct, only a person with DCD would pull away when another person is holding a sharp object in their skin. It tears her cheek. Blood seeps out of it, and Dex still doesn't let go. Instead, he pulls it while it's still attached to her, not letting go until the very end, leaving open gashes behind.

This is the beginning of a masterpiece.

Karen grabs at her injured side, screaming in pain. Dex takes it as an opportunity to do the exact same on the other side. Which he does perfectly.

It's magical to watch him at work.

It is truly a skill. You are either born with it or not.

Jasper walks up to the couch, hopping on the far side. He grabs Karen's arms, holding her wrists in his hand, forcing her to rotate her body to be laying down flat on it. Dex takes the notepad, tearing off a few sheets, then sits on her torso. One by one, he slices the webbing between each of her fingers.

"Dexy, you are doing so good. Such a good boy for Mama." I encourage while watching in awe. He smiles up at me, proud as the day he called me Mama for the first time.

He refocuses on Karen, and slices paper cuts all along her face, including her nostrils and lips. Those two split open almost immediately with blood slowly rising and building around the cuts. Once done with that, the scissors are next.

Doc starts panicking, making terrible whining noises. "Henry, hush. Remember, you're just an observer. This is my session."

Refocusing on the scene before me, Dex is already using the scissors on Karen. He has begun cutting a gaping hole in both her cheeks. Using the punctures left from the staple remover as his starting point.Tears are running down her cheeks. Wait, are they still cheeks if they have holes in them? I am honestly shocked she hasn't passed out from the pain yet. Blood is running down Dex's hands.

"Ris, this is our do-over, don't you think?" Jasper suggests. And I think he's right. We didn't get to have this much fun with mother and father. They were two people who also tried to change us, to separate us, and tried to do something terrible to me... like Henry and Karen did to Dex.

"I think you're right, brother." Smirking at him with my response.

I see Dex making slice marks on Karen's neck, four on each side like fish gills. How clever.

Turning around to face Henry, I grab the letter opener and pull it out of his tongue. I have an idea.

There was one thing I wish we did that we didn't get the chance to do last time. And knowing how Dex likes to play with his toys before ending them, we have time. Plus the door is locked… the finale should just be wrapping up. I think we should have time for this.

Clenching the opener in my fist, I turn around and stab it through Doc's ear into his head. I stab him viciously several more times. Blood is running out of his ear, more each time I stab him. Once I'm done with this ear, I move to the other and do the same thing to that side. Tears are falling from his wide eyes.

He is crying, "Why?"

Before we say goodbye, I tell him exactly why. "You let that vile woman come in here and influence you. You got your dick sucked, fell for her tricks and let her try to change how we run our home. You let her and her sidekicks try to control us. Try to limit us! YOU AND YOUR MERRY CREW DRUGGED AND TORTURED DEX! YOU USED HIM TO PUNISH US! YOU'RE THE SICK ONES. That is why. Everything was just fine, but you went and ruined it. You ruined everything! And like you always told me when I was sent down to the basement, there are always consequences." I scream at him. He is why. He forced us to do this. Everything that's happened is his fault.

Taking the opener, I end it. Stabbing him relentlessly anywhere it will go in. His throat, his chest... I just want him to fucking die!

Jasper's hand comes into my vision; he has the scissors Dex was using clenched in his fist. He joins me in the mayhem. Stabbing Henry in the chest where his lungs are. A giant rush of blood leaves his mouth. This is it. We both stop and let Henry drown in his own blood.

I drop the opener to the floor and look up at Jasper. He follows suit, dropping his scissors. His dick is hard, pressed against his jeans, just begging me to take it out. To fuck in the blood of our enemies.

Seven eight... There is no time to waste.

22

JASPER

That was exhilarating.

Ris and I are covered in a mixture of dried and fresh blood from all who deserved it.

I left Dex to handle Karen. She finally passed out from shock. When she did, I checked her pulse to be sure. Dex is continuing his precise incisions on her while she is still alive. He's gone back to the paper, slowly slicing under only the first couple layers of skin on her arms.

Leaving Dex to it, I grab Savage off the now very dead Doc, and throw her over my shoulder, and she squeals. Taking a few steps to the desk, I place her down to sit on it; her legs hang over the edge and her doe-eyes look up at me between her lashes.

Admiring her body, from her sneaker-clad feet, up

her covered legs and blood soaked bare arms to her perky tits and plump lips. "So fucking beautiful like this, Savage." I mumble under my breath.

She is absolutely stunning.

Time is not on our side, and I am not about to waste any more of it just standing here.

As I reach to remove Ris' shirt, she must have the same thought as me because she reaches for the button of my jeans. She finishes undoing them and raises her arms so I can take her top off over her head, leaving her breasts exposed and her nipples hard. Lowering my head, I take one in my mouth. Savage grabs ahold of my hair as I suck on it, flicking it a couple times with my tongue before nipping it with my teeth, hard. As I do this, she pulls on my hair and arches her back, "Jasp…" she moans. Even how she says my name is hot. I nip at her once more before pulling back, licking my lips which taste of coppery blood. The only thing that would make it better was if her cum was mixed with it. Undoing her pants, Ris leans back on her arms, lifts her ass for me so I can begin pulling them off and down her legs, tossing them to the floor.

No bra and no panties. I swear this girl is trying to kill me.Fuck.

Dropping to my knees, she spreads her legs wide.

Her delicious white thighs invite me in. I take a deep breath; she smells of violence and madness. Two of my favorite things. Inching forward, I begin licking the inside of her thigh, starting at her knee and slowly moving up her soft skin. "Hmm, Jasper. I need more." She begs. I love when my slut begs for me. Not giving into her though, I reach my hand up and grab her exposed, bare pussy and squeeze it. Digging my nails into her skin, she goes to close her legs, but I bite her instead as a warning. I am not done yet. She hisses from the sensation of it all.

"Slut, don't make me stop." I threaten. "No, Jasper. I'll be your pretty little slut and behave... for now." She giggles as I finish making my way with my tongue up her leg to her dripping pussy. Diving right in, I begin lapping her wet lips, getting all her salty delicious juices in my mouth. Moving both my arms under her spread legs, I hook them around her and pull her forward, closer to me. "Suffocate me with your pussy. Cum all over my fucking face, slut." I demand as I begin sucking on her clit. I feel her fingers in my hair again, and her nails dig into my skull as I begin to suck harder and her legs start to tremble. Ris starts using my face, rubbing her pussy against it, chasing her own release. Using my tongue again, I play with her swollen lips, just to toy with her. To make her even more needy to cum, to drown me in her release.

Giving in, I flick her clit with my tongue now, getting her closer to what she desires. Then, before I allow her to cum, I bite down on her sensitive nub. Savage's nails dig harder into my skull as she moans into the room. Using my face once more, she rubs herself on me as I suck her harder, and Ris's whole body trembles as she cums in my mouth. Her salty, creamy release and the coppery blood mix together, and it tastes like fucking heaven. It enrages me that some is dripping down my chin. I need it all. Devouring her until I get every last drop.

As her orgasm begins to fade, I realize I can feel my own heart beating rapidly inside my chest. Savage cumming turns me into a fucking fiend.

Standing up, I can see Savage's head is thrown back and her eyes are closed. Her chest is moving rapidly while sweat runs down her face, causing the dried blood on her forehead to glisten. I pull my pants down to my ankles, my boxers follow and my hard cock springs up with precum already dripping from my head. Ris, who is now focused on me, grabs *her* cock, massaging the tip with her thumb a couple times before bringing it to her mouth, sucking me off of her.

"My beautiful Savage, covered in blood, sucking my cum off your fingers. Fucking perfect." I rasp at her with hooded eyes. Then I line my cock up with her entrance, rubbing my tip around it, before slamming into her. Reaching up, I take my hand and wrap it around her neck. Our vows aligned, Mine and Yours. We will always be one depraved soul split into two bodies, connected forever, even after death tries to separate us.

"Choke me, Jasp. I want to see the stars." Savage whimpers as I continue to thrust my cock into her pussy. Squeezing her throat tighter, she parts her lips, but she keeps her eyes locked on me. "That's my good little slut. Keep those pretty eyes on me when I pound into your tight pussy." This praise makes her smile, as her eyes become more hooded from a mixture of ecstasy and lack of oxygen. Using my other hand, I grab her tiny breast in my hand and squeeze it as tight as I can, and a raspy moan escapes her. Fucking beautiful. The power I have; that she gives me. It's one of the greatest gifts one can be given. Her hands are holding onto the edge of the desk, to stop her from moving with each movement I make, which are becoming faster as I feel my own orgasm starting to build.

Fucking her harder and faster with each movement, my cock rubs against the walls of her tight pussy. As it's about to hit me, Savage's eyes completely close, her hold on the desk loosens, "Cum for your brother. Cum now, slut." I demand as my own release hits. Letting go of her throat and breast, I move my hands to her hips. Holding on to her as I work us through it, ropes of my warm cum coating her insides.

Ris gasps as she regains consciousness, her legs wrap around me and she rakes her nails down my bloody, shirt-clad chest. She trembles as she obeys me, cumming all over my cock. We share the same blood, and our cum is mixing together inside of her. No other human in this world, at this moment, can say they are closer than we are. Right now.

Pulling her closer, I press her against me, soaking her chest with the blood still wet on my shirt. Kissing her swollen lips, my tongue invades her mouth. I will never get enough of her. Ever.

My cock is still inside of her, and if we didn't need to get moving, I would go for round two right fucking now.

Pulling back, I break the kiss. Ris pulls back and examines her crimson chest. "Beautiful." She whispers in admiration.

Ris grabs my face with both her hands and with absolute certainty says, "I love you, Jasp. Always."

Resting my forehead against hers, "I know Savage. I would fucking die for you. Fight for you. Live for you. I love you so much."

She kisses me once more and mumbles against my lips, "We should get dressed. Dexy shouldn't see me like this."

Fuck.

She's not wrong.

I pull my cock out of her warm pussy, and our cum leaks out instantly. It's a fucking incredible sight, watching it slowly drip down her thigh. Looking to the ground, I find her shirt that I threw, and her pants and help her get dressed. She puts her arms up, and I pull her top down over her. She holds her legs up and I slide her pants up her legs until she takes over, jumping off the desk to bring them over her peachy ass. I reach down and bring my own pants up, doing them up and turn around to see Dex still hovering over Karen, hard at work.

The guy created a goddamn masterpiece while we were busy fucking, covered in Doc's blood.

He has covered her arms, face, and neck in small half-circle cuts. You can see her blood through the thin pieces. It reminds me of scales on a fish.

Ris steps around me, gasping with her hands over her mouth in awe. "Dexy, this is magnificent."

He turns his head, smiling with pride.

"Dexy, you know. We still have to kill her, right? I can't let her live for what she did to you down in that basement. What she did to us when she took you."

He nods his head. He knows.

Ris walks over to Karen, "Bitch, WAKE UP!" Screaming while slapping her face.

"You will not sleep through your own death! It's rude! We have been waiting forever for this."

Karen looks down at her body and notices all the cuts, and starts screaming. I don't think the pain has registered with her yet.

Dex takes matters into his own hands, standing to pick up the scissors I tossed after killing Doc. He starts stabbing her repeatedly, in the chest, the neck and stomach. Blood is streaming out of Karen's mouth. She is coughing, which tells me she's a goner. Blood is filling her lungs, replacing the air and drowning her. Dex stabs her twice more in the heart, then drops the scissors on top of her.

Savage is captivated by the scene before her. I walk over to Dex, and put my hand on his shoulder, reassuring him it was the right thing. It had to happen. He just nods in understanding.

The three of us are standing around looking at Karen when a knock interrupts us.

Another frantic knock on the door causes us to look towards it and this time it's followed by a guy shouting.

"Doctor Peters, Doctor Peters! You got to get out here! The basements unlocked, there's blood and Beth... Beth she's... she's dead!"

Pussy.

'Breaking News! This just in. We already know Susan is dead, fuck head.
And surprise, the guy you're crying for is too.'

Savage is speaking her thoughts again. Fuck, I love her crazy. Then she clears her throat, which causes Dex and I to turn to look at her.

Ris is standing by the speaker phone device next to Doc's chair, where he is slumped over.

She presses the intercom button, gives us a wink and begins, "Hello Sutton, this is your prom Queen!"

Nine Ten... Now is your time for your revenge...

Residents of Sutton.

23

IRIS

"Hello Sutton, this is your prom Queen! That's right! We are finally getting the prom we have been dreaming of.

This year's theme is Blood, Murder and Mayhem!"

Finally, this is my moment. I couldn't have pictured a better prom even if I'd tried.

"We may not have much time, as one of those dicks may have called for reinforcements. But we will celebrate while we can. So, stop just standing there and let's fucking party!" I'm so excited, even the residents from the secure wing are able to join us.

"We do have some special guests joining us from the secure wing. Meet us in Henry's office because… Dinner is served!" I click the intercom button again to turn it off. Now I know what you're thinking, *"Iris,*

221

how generous of you." Well, of course, I cannot be labeled a bad host. The least I can do is provide them with something to eat.

"Dexy, Jasp, can you please unlock and open the door? I would hate to keep them waiting and their food goes bad."

Dexy has his own art piece decorated on him now, compliments of Karen. The three of us are absolutely stunning. As I admire Dex, Jasper unlocks the door, so it's open for when our secure wing friends arrive. As soon as it opens, the sound that was previously blocked out invades the space. You hear loud screams of terror, mixed in with laughter. It sounds like everyone is having the best time! And right on cue, a couple of residents walk in for their open buffet.

"Welcome. Thank you for joining us! My name is Iris, that's Jasper and my baby boy Dexy. It's a pleasure to meet you all. We have prepared you these delicious bodies for your enjoyment. Please dig in! Wait! I forgot... dessert is in the basement. Don't forget about dessert, ok?"

If I had forgotten to tell them about dessert, they would have given me a terrible review, I'm sure of it.

As the secure wing digs in, I start to walk towards the door when Ms. O appears. "Ms.O, I had no idea. Please help yourself. This evening we have two main options, Doctor Peters or Karen. Dessert is in the basement." This is so exciting! She must have hid this from everyone, otherwise she surely would have ended up in the secure wing.

"Thank you, Ms. Iris." Oh my word, she said my name! Usually, she just nods or smiles at me. I am such a fan. It's officially the best night ever.

Giddy with excitement, I want to join the others and experience prom properly. "Let's go boys!" I holler at both of them as I walk around Ms. O and head into the hallway. Then I remember, "Oh! There's Vicodin on the floor by Karen. Feel free to have that for your appetizer or a palate cleanser, if you'd like." Shouting back in the room filled with our new friends. I am definitely getting a five star review. This is first class treatment, and the freshest of ingredients for them.

Walking down the hall with my boys, the sound of absolute chaos and mayhem grows louder.

Then it hits me. I don't know how Greys ended. Shit, I hope someone recorded it for me. It was worth missing though. I mean, look at this beautiful sight.

The staff have looks of terror on their faces, while some try to contain what's erupting, others run away from it. Patients rush out behind them as they leave the TV room. Some have jumped over the nurses' station and have begun ransacking the desks and cabinets. I'm sure others have also hit up the meds station. How could they not? It's like the ultimate candy store. A few are leaning against the wall and watching everything happen.

The only thing that could make this night better would be some killer music and lights.

Besides that, this is the best prom ever!

Pulling on Jasper's arm, I stare up at him, still amazed that we pulled this prom off. "Look at this. We did this. We made our kingdom happy. This is the greatest feeling."

Smiling back down at me, he says. "Savage, you did this. You are their fucking queen and you helped turn this place into the most incredible madhouse. They fucked with our family and you grabbed them by the balls and made them your bitch. They paid in screams and skin. We only helped you achieve this. You hold the power with us, Savage. Your wish is always our command. You empower everyone around you to be their most authentic selves and embrace their crazy. It takes a rare, special person to have these abilities, but you do. We fucking love you, Savage."

Dex comes up behind me and wraps his arms around my shoulders and kisses the side of my head, and Jasper grabs my head and kisses my lips. Dammit, these guys are trying to make me feel and shit. And it could be working.

"Now, let's finish this. What do you say, Savage?"

Blinking a few times quickly, I must get this annoying water out of my eyes. I yell, "Yes!"

Letting go of Jasper's arm, I turn in place and give Dexy the biggest hug. I have missed this man. My boy.

"Thank you, Dexy. I almost lost you. I almost lost myself when you were gone. Then I remembered, we can't let these fuckers win. We run this place. We own our home. Mama loves you, always. Now let's go out with a bang. What do you say?" I can feel him nodding, then he holds me tighter, whispering, "Mama" into my neck. That's all I need.

We let go of each other, still looking absolutely deranged, covered in blood with mischievous smiles on our faces. I am so excited!

Once Dexy lets go of me, I see his eyes shifting, as if he is looking for someone. Hmm, what are you up to, mister?

His eyes stop and focus in on someone. As they do, he taps Jasper on the shoulder and points. Jasper looks over, nods his head once without even looking back at Dexy, and yells. "Joseph! Come here."

Oh, the plot thickens. What are these boys up to?

I turn around to watch. Curiosity only kills cats, and thankfully, I'm not one.

Reaching into his front pocket, Jasp pulls something out and keeps it in his hand.

"Take this," he tells Joseph, who looks confused, but still reaches his hand out.

Jasper tosses the lighter at Joseph. His eyes light up. "Wow, Jasper. Thank you. Thank you, man." Joseph is speechless, it's like we have just given him the prom king title and instead of a crown it's his favorite thing, a lighter… Fire.

All Jasper says in response is, "Light it up." One simple but exhilarating instruction. Fitting perfectly with our theme of this evening.

"We are having a bonfire. We are having a bonfire," I chant while clapping my hands together. I think I'm as excited as Joseph. Who is now grinning ear to ear. "You got it." Is all he says before taking off to the library.

Oh no, those poor books. The thought of them burning in the flames makes me sad for a few seconds. But I quickly get over it. Saluting no one in particular, "Thank you for your sacrifices books. We thank you and we will never forget you." Then drop my hand down. That's when it hits me. Shit, what about Mr. H?

"Wait, Jasper. Make sure someone helps Mr. H, please." I plead with my brother. He nods his head and whistles at one of Joseph's friends to get their attention. "You. Make sure Mr. H gets out. Got it?" The guy looks terrified of Jasp. "Yes, of course, sir. Whatever you need, sir." Sir? No, Jasper is more like a daddy.

"Then go!" Jasp barks at him. Daddy Jasper means business.

Once he's gone, Jasper looks down at me, smiling. "Never change, Savage." Then kisses my forehead, "You said '*Daddy Jasper means business*' out loud," he chuckles.

People are still running chaotically around us. I wish I had a camera to capture these special moments. A voice screeches, "Someone open the door! Please, who has a key?" We turn to where the voice is coming from. It's a female aide, and she is crying with her face blotchy red. We have bars blocking the door. Someone would have to unlock those doors in order to get the front doors, or any other door here, open. Jasper whispers in my ear, "When we leave, it will be through those back doors. Not the front."

I understand what he's saying. Everyone will rush

to the front, and we can sneak out the back completely undetected. This night just keeps getting better and better.

"Now, son. I do not like leaving my room. They do not like me leaving my room."

Mr. H states.

Turning around, I see him walking down the stairs reluctantly. "Mr. H, don't worry. You will not want to miss this. I promise."

"Oh, Iris. This is all so strange. You know how I get overstimulated. I can't promise I will behave."

"Good, just what this party needs!" I feel relieved that he's down here. He has been like a father figure to us. If this place burns, at least I know he's going to be safe. And I know what you're all thinking, ew gross, you fuck in front of him and you consider him a father figure? Newsflash people— fuck my twin brother, too.

"I have a key! Let me through you disgusting creatures!" A voice that sounds like they have smoked twelve packs a day since birth catches my attention. What did he just call us?

No one calls us that. NO ONE!

He is an older nurse, a miserable bastard. I walk up to him and grab him by the neck of his scrubs and get right in his face. "We are NOT disgusting creatures. And by the looks of it, we run this house, not you! So you watch what you fucking say to us. Now apologize!"

He stays silent. Come on, old man, make the right decision.

"No."

Just as he says it, a sharp, thick piece of wood—I think it's a chair leg—shoots out of his face, blood splatters on me and I let go, letting him drop to the ground.

Ah, it's one of my restaurant's buffet attendees. "Thank you, kind sir." And I take a bow as a sign of respect.

"Of course, m'lady queen" He says back, bowing as well before walking away.

What a nice guy!

I smell it before I see it. Smoke. Joseph is playing!

The alarms haven't gone off yet. And I know we can open the doors, but it would only cause more pandemonium. Jasper's right, we have to be smart about this.

Stepping over Mr. Grumpy Pants who is very dead on the ground, I see Dex and Jasper are also on the move, motioning me to come over to them.

As I do, Joseph runs out from the hallway,

which leads to the library. "Guys. She's a big one. Get ready!" His eyes are dilated, eyes are hooded, and I would swear he just got fucked if he didn't smell like smoke. I think he just loves fire that much.

His white hair has dark ashes on the tips and his long-sleeved shirt is rolled up his arms. He means business. I appreciate that. Joseph is given a task, and he doesn't fuck around. He would make a good knight in our kingdom.

Within seconds of him saying that, and being lost in my own thoughts, the alarms start blaring. Red lights are strobing around the room and this machine voice is saying, '*Fire. Fire. Fire.*'

My body starts moving to the rhythm. This is our final song of the night.

Ok residents, it's time to go! You don't have to scurry home, but you no longer have to stay here.

Over the commotion and our new soundtrack, you can faintly hear the bars at the front doors click and slide open automatically as a part of the fire alarm system. People start rushing it, and the aide who was pleading for us to unlock it earlier is the first through. She wiggles the front door handle a few times before it opens. A group follows after her, going outside to escape the smoke and fire.

I feel soft hands slide into both of mine, it's Dex and Jasper. It's go time baby!

Dex leads. I'm behind him and Jasper is behind me. We maneuver through people going the opposite direction of us. A couple see what we are doing and turn around, following behind us. Passing the nurses' desk now, we are almost there.

We pass through the opening where the barred door was, and Dex pushes the wooden backdoor open. The smell of fresh air enters my lungs. It's been weeks since I've smelled any air except for the stale air inside.

"Jasper. The fence. We are fenced in!" I'm not one to panic, but I think maybe we should have found another exit. Lining the top of the fence is barbed wire. There is no fucking way I am climbing over that. I love pain as much as the next person, but I think I just found my boundary.

"Ris, calm down. There's a gate in the fence in the back corner. It has to open. How could it not? You can't keep people locked in this cage with a fire. Dex, keep going. DO. NOT. STOP." Jasper demands. I just hope he's right. Emergency lights illuminate the area closest to the house. As we get further away, it gets darker and darker. My eyes slowly adjust, and I can faintly see what Jasper is talking about. We pass some

231

trees and a bench, before finally reaching the gate. We stop in front of it and Dex turns it slowly, building the suspense. Fucker. Please be unlocked. Please. It has to be. If it isn't, we are completely screwed. You can hear the sirens getting closer.

No, no, not again. We cannot be caught again. We were like this last time. Covered in blood. Holding each other after killing mother and father when the sirens came and they took us away. This is just like that night.

Please be unlocked. They will separate us. We can't be separated. My breathing picks up. I can't be away from them.

"They won't get us, Savage." Jasper whispers in my ear at the same time we hear a click and Dex pushes the gate open. Dex pulls on my hand as he walks through it, and I pull on Jasper's to follow us. As we cross the threshold, all I can think of is freedom. We finally have our freedom.

An unfamiliar voice catches our attention. I'd almost forgotten these people followed us out. "So what now?" They ask.

"I don't think so. I don't give a fuck where you go, but you're not coming with us. So get the fuck out of here. NOW!" Jasper snaps at them. I'm sure they shit themselves. When Jasper means business, he doesn't play nice. His tone says it all.

"Uh, ya. Ok. You're right. Let's split up." Fuckhead murmurs back, like it was his idea.

"Then go!"

They take off into the dark without another word.

"We have to move. It won't take them long to do a head count and notice we are gone. Fuck, someone is bound to rat on the whole thing. They will be scouring the entire fucking town and county for us." Jasper sighs, while brushing his fingers through his hair.

This is it. We are almost home free.

DAYS LATER

JASPER

We have been walking for days. And I pray to fuck we are still walking in the right direction. Sticking to the thick tree line makes it hard to tell. But hearing the stream a few yards away reassures me it has to be fucking right.

The first night after we escaped, we walked until sunrise, not stopping once. The moon was the only light we had moving through the thick bush and trees. We needed to get as far away from Sutton as we could.

At one point we heard dogs barking, and I can only assume they were there for us, trying to find our scent and hunting us. We'd kept our blood-soaked clothing on. Our logic being, it would cover our scent up enough that the dogs would only be able to smell the blood of our playthings; Doc, the aides and Karen.

There is no fucking way cops would have waved their blood in front of the dogs and yell go find them. Keeping them on was our best bet in getting out forever.

Once the sun started coming up, we were fucking exhausted. Ris was walking behind us when we heard a splash. That was her telling us she was done. She found a pond and jumped in, fully clothed. Once she came up from under the water, she demanded, "We are resting. We are washing. I need a break. My feet are killing me, Jasp. Please."

Savage sounded defeated. She never shows this side, ever. So the one time she does, I wasn't going to question it or pressure her. Instead, I walked to the edge of the pond and jumped in, too. Dex followed.

We cleaned ourselves off, eventually getting out, hanging our clothes to dry in the hot North Carolina heat and rested. Letting Dex and Ris sleep first, I stayed up to keep watch. We had made it this far; we are not going back. Hours passed, I could tell from watching the sun move across the sky through the trees. At one point, Dex woke up, and he took watch while I slept with my Savage.

By the time I woke, the sun was down, and Dex and Savage were up and dressed. A pile of blackberries in front of them. "Hey Jasp, we found some food." Ris offers. Fuck, she's beautiful.

Smiling back at her, I sit up and grab a few to eat.

"Let me get dressed and we can keep going."

We lived like this for days. Would walk as far as we could before collapsing. Ris would argue that she could take a watch while we slept, but we never let her win. She freed us. Now it was our turn to let her rest and recharge because who fucking knew what the next day would bring. We needed her ready.

It's night now. The stream is still alongside us. After the first night, we hadn't heard dogs since. There also weren't any search lights from the sky that we had to hide from. I wonder if we got lucky, and they started searching in the opposite direction. But I was not about to question it.

Fuck, we have to be getting closer. Sutton and our old family home were only a few hours' drive apart. It had a stream behind it, and I prayed to Satan the stream we were following was the same one. There is no way the cops or authorities would be waiting for us at the house. What reason would we have to go back, right?

"Jasper, where are we going?" Ris asks for the twentieth time today.

Laughing at her, as I walk ahead, "Savage, you'll

see. I think we're almost there." All she does is growl back at me, accepting my answer. We walk a few more yards when an area of the stream seems familiar to me.

"Stay here, hold on." I tell both of them, as I run closer to the edge, out of the treeline. Looking around, fuck yes, I see the clearing lit by the moon and stars of the night. We are back!

"Guys, we're here!"

Both come up behind me to see what I'm talking about. It takes Ris seconds to realize where we are when she gasps, "Jasper. No way! You're a fucking wizard. How did you know what direction to go?" She is in complete shock and disbelief.

We are back in South Carolina.

"I just fucking hoped, honestly. It just felt right going this way." I explain, looking at Dex, he still seems confused on what the fuss is about.

"Dexy, this was our home," Ris explains. "But why did we come here? I don't understand."

"Come on, I'll explain on the way."

We take off towards the open field where our giant white house sits. No lights are on from what I can tell. Which is a good sign for what I am about to do.

"Dex, can I borrow your hoodie?" I ask. He has it

wrapped around his neck, but he undoes it and passes it over.

In case there are cameras I don't want them catching my face, the hood should hide it.

As we get closer to the house, something seems off. There isn't anything out on the patio, and the pool looks empty with vines and overgrown grass surrounding it. What the fuck?

"Jasp, I think the windows are boarded up. See, there's dark wood over all of them." She points.

This could be a good sign. I don't have to worry about a family waking up when I break in. But if whoever boarded up this place searched it, I mean really searched it before doing so. Then this was all for nothing.

"I need you both to stay here. Ris, I fucking mean it. Don't move. Even if someone comes up to the house while I'm in it. Let me go." Instructing both of them.

"Not a chance, brother. You are family and we don't leave family behind." Ris snaps back.

"Can you just tell me what I want to hear, regardless if you listen to it or not, please."

"Oh, sure, yes daddy Jasper. I'll be a good little girl and stay here just like you asked. And if I should move, I could only hope you punish me thoroughly later." Such a fucking brat.

Chuckling, "Thank you. I'll be right back." And with that, I take off into the field and make my way to the backdoor. It's also boarded up, but the bottom is missing a few. I bet teens and shit come up here because I also faintly see spray paint along them. Slipping through the opening, I'm in the kitchen where it all happened. It takes a moment for my eyes to adjust, and I can see there isn't any furniture left. I can't tell if they cleaned up the blood, but I can only assume so if everything else is gone. I remember this place like it was yesterday. I could maneuver through it with my eyes closed, which is good because I can't see shit in here.

As I walk through the place, I kick some bottles I didn't see. Kids definitely party here. Finding the stairs, I make my way up them, and they squeak with each step I take. That's new.

Shit, I hope these kids didn't find shit here, either. It has to be here. Please let it still be here. I know we haven't been saints, but please let this work out and it still be here. Down the hall, I touch the walls and feel the wallpaper which is torn and falling off, but it still smells the same. Maybe just a little bit more stale from lack of fresh air.

Passing Savage's old room, then mine, I briefly peek into both as I pass. The cracks in the boards allow some moonlight to come through, and I see both rooms are empty. Then, walking a bit further, I approach my mother and father's room. My heart is beating rapidly now. Worry filling my head.

Stepping through the open door, I try to not let the memories of this place flood my mind. There were some good ones, with Savage, but most of the memories are horrid. Quickly, I head to their walk-in closet, where it has white built-in shelves and cabinets, it even has a center island in it. Bypassing it, I head to the back row of shelving and begin pushing on them. One of them has a secret storage door. I only know this because I followed father in here one day. He had a duffle bag over his shoulder and he pushed the shelving and it popped open where he threw the bag in.

Father was a slimy motherfucker. No one who works with the church has the money we do. So the only thing that could be in that bag is cash. Or shit you can trade for it. Frantically, I keep pushing on each shelf and hope it opens, but it doesn't. I am at the last two on the bottom of the wall now and push it hard. Come on, fucking open. First hearing the click, then it pops open slightly.

Thank fuck. I sigh in relief.

Opening it fully, I reach my arm in and start patting around. Please be here. The hole is deep and I end up having to put my leg in it to reach my body further in. The dust is making my eyes water, even causing me to sneeze a few times. Then I feel it, the fabric strap. Wrapping my fingers around it, I pull it towards me, then lift it up and throw it over my shoulder. It's not overly heavy, which worries me, but I don't care right now. I found it and now I have to get out of here.

Closing the hidden door, I rush out of the room, wasting no time.

Making my way back down the hall, I grab onto the stair railing as I rush down them. Making my way back through the kitchen to the backdoor I kneel down, throwing the bag through first and I follow. Picking it back up, I make a mad dash through the open field back to the treeline where Ris and Dex are waiting for me.

Making it back to them within seconds, I'm out of breath as I drop the bag in front of them.

"Jasp, shit. What is this?" Ris asks.

Still trying to recover, I say through each breath. "Open. It."

Dex kneels down and begins unzipping the bag. All three of us are waiting with anticipation.

Once unzipped, Dex widens the opening of the bag. Ris is the first to say anything, it's one word, but it says it all.

"Shit."

EPILOGUE

IRIS

A FEW YEARS LATER

S tanding outside in the hot Georgia heat, I'm in a pair of high-waisted blue jean shorts and a white tube top. My long black hair is up in a messy bun, my feet are bare against the earth. We have been here for a couple years now, making it into our home, and I fucking love it.

Now, I know what you're wondering.

What was in the bag?

Wouldn't you like to know.

"Savage, just tell them." Jasper hollers at me from inside the old abandoned barn we have turned into ours, with my Dexy, of course.

Fine, I'll tell you. It was cash. A lot of fucking cash.

Remember, father worked for the 'Church.'

Even from the dead, they are still gifting their killer children with their fortunes. We haven't used a lot of it. Not wanting to be seen in public. We aren't sure if we are still being looked for, if people will see us and report back to the police. I refuse to let them take us!

We walked for over a week after stopping back at the ol' family home before finding this place. The barn is abandoned in the brush, and has overgrown greenery all over it. We never cleared it off, as we didn't want anyone to think we had taken up residence. Although inside we have tidied it. Beds made of hay we found in fields at night. We would also make our rounds at camp sites, taking a few things we needed at a time, not wanting to draw any suspicion. Over the years, we have collected enough to make it feel comfortable.

Dex went into town one day and bought a few things for him and Jasper. We figured no one would recognize him or bother him based on his size. They would be too scared to. There is a small farmhouse an hour out, and a girl my age lives there. So I broke into her room and took a few things for myself. I still do from time to time as I need things. I'm sure she notices, but no one has ever come looking down here for us. So we still have a lot of cash.

Jasper and I even fucked in the cash once we got here. Just one more fuck you to mother and father. I came all over it. Soaking a few bills enough with my cum that they tore apart.

Fuck, now I'm horny!

"Jasper! Look what you did. Now I'm horny thinking about that night with the money." I stomp and walk over to the open door of the barn, pouting.

"On your knees, slut. Suck my cock. That should help," Jasper demands. Oh, daddy Jasper is here!

"Yes, he is." He responds. Fuck. I said it out loud again.

We are on a mission, so I waste no time dropping to my knees on the hard ground as he walks towards me, closing the gap between us. Jasper pulls his shorts down and his hard cock springs out.

My mouth begins to salivate at the sight. His cock is the most beautiful thing I have ever seen.

Jasp holds it up to my mouth with one hand and with his other places it at the back of my head and pushes my open mouth onto him. His tip hits the back of my throat and I gag. He loves when I gag. I swear it's his mission to make me vomit on it. Which could very well happen from him shoving his giant shaft down my throat with such force.

Drool trails down my lips onto my chin as he continues to face fuck me. My eyes water, and it's getting harder to catch a breath.

Raising my hands, I brace myself using his thighs and look up at him through my eyelashes.

"So fucking beautiful. MINE. Only ever MINE." He rasps with hooded eyes looking back down at me.

Mumbling over his dick, "Yours."

This sends him into a frenzy. His movements get quicker and harder. I fucking live for this!

My lips meet his pelvis now with each thrust into my mouth. Jasper is all the way down my throat. I own him. He owns me.

I gag a couple more times, and I begin to feel the warm ropes of his salty cum beginning to coat my throat. Jasper doesn't let up. Still assaulting me with his movements. "Fuck, Savage. Fucking take it!" He barks at me.

And I do. I take every ounce, every drop.

His movements start to become less frantic. He removes his hand from my hair and I begin to slowly pull back. His cock coming out of my mouth as I clean it off with my tongue and lips at the same time.

I love his taste.

Jasper smiles down at me with pride, "You did so good, Savage." His thumb wipes the tears that were trailing down my cheek.

Before his cock is fully out of my mouth, I suck on his tip and circle it with my tongue. I know exactly what I'm doing.

Jasper reaches down and grabs my throat with his hand and squeezes it. He pulls his dick out of my mouth and pulls me up off my knees.

Smiling at him, with my drool mixed with some of his cum dripping down my chin, he smashes his lips onto mine. Jasper's tongue invades my mouth. I'm sure he is also tasting himself or what is left of him from my tongue. He squeezes my neck a bit more, and bites my lip at the same time, grumbling against them, "MINE!"

Smiling back at him, trying to suck air into my lungs and whisper, "Yours!"

"Good." Is all he says back before letting me go.

I don't clean my chin. I keep our mixture glistening off of it. I love feeling him on my skin whatever way I can get it. Although, I do brush the dirt off my knees, left behind from kneeling on the ground.

Once I catch my breath, "Jasp, we should get going." He nods back to me as he pulls his pants up, then holds his hand out as if to say *lead the way*. Spinning around, I do!

We have noticed Dexy has been going missing for hours at a time lately. Me, being my curious self, couldn't not follow him almost every time after we noticed.

Skipping through the trees, I can hear birds singing above us. Wild flowers are growing, and butterflies flutter. I really love it here. I hope we don't ever have to move. It does keep my mind more peaceful being out here.

Don't worry, not completely. How boring would that be?

As we get closer to where Dex is, I turn around with my finger against my lips. "Shh. We are almost there."

Focusing in front of me again, I watch each of my steps. The minute we step on a twig or leaves ruffle under our feet. We are so busted.

We are here.

Dex is sitting on a big rock on the ground. I hold my arm up so Jasper knows to stop once he gets next to me, which he does.

We both watch him for a while. I have told Jasper what I've seen out here, but he has never seen it for himself. This is very exciting!

Then in the meadow before us, a girl appears. The same girl I steal from.

She is maybe our age, early twenties. With soft red hair in a high ponytail, wearing a thin white lace top and blue jean shorts. You can see freckles on her nose and under her eyes. She has thin lips and a tiny frame with green eyes that pop against her pale skin. This girl is absolutely stunning. No wonder Dex is smitten by her. I look over at him and his head is now resting on his hands as he watches her pick the wild flowers. She places a couple daisies in her hair, but keeps the rest in a bunch in her hand.

I wonder what her name is.

She does seem too sweet for us. What if my Dexy wants her, but she gets scared of him? Doesn't accept him for him and all his demons.

Who are we fooling? I'd kill the bitch. If it came to it.

We should get going before Dex notices us.

But before we go, I get an idea. This is the best fucking idea since Karen!

I turn to Jasper and stand on my tippy toes and whisper into his ear,

"Jasper, I have an idea!"

A few days later, we call Dex in and open the cold storage container we have in the ground.

I'm so fucking excited. I hope he likes his present!

Jasper is next to me, standing still while waiting for Dexy. But not me. I am vibrating with anticipation.

Bouncing on the balls of my feet now as he walks in through the barn doors. His face is amused by my energy.

Once he is in front of me, I point down through the hole and yell,

"SURPRISE!"

DEX

IT'S HER!

THE END…
… of Iris and Jasper Ashford's story.
Stay Tuned, Queens!

Dex's Story 'Sick Obsession' is Releasing Sometime in 2024.

ACKNOWLEDGEMENTS

Where Lily was a slight representation of my Mental Health side. Iris Ashford is my Harley Quinn soul. You should note. I may think things but I would never act on them like our dear Savage does. I like my freedom. Jail doesn't scream 'it's a great time' to me. Well unless it's the haunted prison in the UK I'll be visiting next year. That shit screams pick me, choose me, love me!

Ok, enough of my rambles.

There was a bit of hype or excitement around Sutton Asylum, and I hope it lived up to your expectations. If not, that's ok too! No hard feelings.

The twins were incredibly fun to write. Iris invaded my thoughts the entire process and I would crave writing her constantly. Jasper was a blast as well. He is dedicated to her for life. He isn't sane by any means, but he keeps her leveled. They balance each other. I absolutely adore the two of them. Then we have our Dexy.

His story is coming. The twins will make appearances. But it will be Dex's journey. I know it will be mentally exhausting writing him and his story. His trauma is dark. It will be very much included in Sick Obsession. It's a part of his life, it's how he ended up in Sutton and it's a part of what made him the Dexy he is today. As horrible as it is, it happened.

The earliest I can see myself starting his book is sometime in the Spring. I need to be able to escape from his darkness and go outside to have the sun shine down on me between chapters. To recharge myself. Yes! It will be Taboo. How? You will have to wait and see!

To you, the Reader - Thank you sooo much for reading! I appreciate every single one of you who have taken a chance on me. Thank you for wanting to be a part of this ride. Thank you for buying my books and cheering me on. THANK YOU, QUEENS!

My Alpha & Beta's. Thank you for pushing me. For providing incredible commentary. You volunteer your free time to help me and I don't take it for granted. Thank you!

ARC and TikTok Team. Ya'll are amazing. Your excitement, gets me excited! Thank you for even wanting to be on my team. It is still so wild to me. I swear there was nothing in the kool-aid we handed out once you entered. But thank you for drinking it!!

The Crafty Book Witch Editor. Rae. Fellow Libra Sister. We see you! Thank you for always taking care of my babies!!

One Click! What more is there to say about this gem? She likes to be clicked, she also does the clicking. The girl is a warrior!

Hayley, because teasing is fun!

Mr. Kincaid. Don't be scared after reading this. It's fine. Everything is fine. You know I'm nuts. So this book was to be expected.

The Oprah to my Gayle. You know who you are. You know how I feel. YOU are never escaping me. Because being bad together is more fun than being good, even if we are wearing Crocs that were hand-crafted by the Frog King.

Until the next one, Queens
-Kins

ABOUT THE AUTHOR

Kinsley is a Canadian, Dark Taboo Romance Author. When she isn't plotting her next twisted book or watching true crime docs with her cats, you can find her working for the man. Reading. Or drinking wine… vodka… beer… while causing chaos with friends, let's not limit ourselves now. Make sure you follow Kins on her socials and sign up for her newsletter to see what is coming next!

authorkinsleykincaid.com

MORE FROM KINSLEY

FORBIDDEN

Let's Play

Within the Shadows

Lessons from the Depraved - Feb 2024

TABOO

Wrecked

Sutton Asylum

Sick Obsession - 2024